5 Reasons We Think You'll Love This Book

Meet Kale and Strife, water voles with a n___ and an eye for adven___

The beautiful illustrations by Simon Mendez will transport you to the Wetted Land.

Packed full of fascinating wildlife facts.

An unforgettable tale of courage and friendship.

A breath of fresh riverside air.

'This book is packed with detail about water voles and their habitat yet the detail never seems forced, enhancing rather than overtaking the story.'

Edd Bankes, Armadillo Magazine

'Ecologist Tom Moorhouse transports us into a colourful world in this follow-up to *The River Singers*.'

BBC Wildlife

'Both gripping and moving.'

Carousel

'It's really really difficult to write animal stories which do justice to the nature of the animal and the human need for a human story . . . Tom Moorhouse has managed to produce yet another compelling story.'

Melanie McDonagh, 'Children's books for Christmas', Spectator

'A beautiful uplifting story full of excitement, lyricism and peril . . . an exceptional series from an exceptional author.'

Pam Norfolk, Lancashire Evening Post

For Sue and Andy

OXFORD
UNIVERSITY PRESS

Great Clarendon Street, Oxford OX2 6DP

Oxford University Press is a department of the University of Oxford.
It furthers the University's objective of excellence in research, scholarship,
and education by publishing worldwide. Oxford is a registered trade mark of
Oxford University Press in the UK and in certain other countries

First published 2014
First published in this paperback edition 2015

British Library Cataloguing in Publication Data

Data available

ISBN: 978-0-19-273483-9

1 3 5 7 9 10 8 6 4 2

Printed and bound by CPI Group (UK) Ltd, Croydon, CR0 4YY

Paper used in the production of this book is a natural,
recyclable product made from wood grown in sustainable forests.
The manufacturing process conforms to the environmental
regulations of the country of origin.

The Rising

Tom Moorhouse

Illustrated by Simon Mendez

OXFORD
UNIVERSITY PRESS

We are River Singers, Water Folk,
children of Sinethis. We live by her ways.
She takes our old and gives us young. She
stirs our hunger, feeds us with grasses.
She shelters us in her waters and burrows.
She rises and dashes us. She sings with
us a song as soft as thistles, hard as roots,
deep as shadows, old as stones. We sing
with her a song as quick as thinking,
sweet as apples, brief as day. We are River
Singers, and we are hers.

PROLOGUE

Rain lashed the Wetted Land. It bent the reeds and flattened the sweet-grass. It poured into the dykes until the water seethed with it. The onslaught was ceaseless: no sound but rain, no colour but grey, and no scent but wetness. The world was rinsed clean of everything else.

It began as a chilly spatter, blown in on a freshening breeze. Youngsters played among the first drops, before heading home. And then it came in earnest. Adults fled for cover, keeping to runs beneath a thick thatch of plants. They shook the water from their fur and sheltered in their burrows. They cast wry looks at the clouds and waited for the rain to pass. But it did not.

After the first days the ground was soaked. Water trickled from every surface. It cascaded from leaves, dripped through cracks, and spread wetly across burrow walls. Floors turned to mud. Bedding grew damp and chilly. Summer chatter dissolved away and squabbles erupted across the marsh. The mood in the Wetted Land soured.

Then the enemies, initially den-bound, came out in numbers to hunt the dyke edges. In the rain they were impossible to hear. Folk were snatched with grasses still in their paws, or dragged from their burrows. The pups grew fearful in their nests. *Don't worry, their mothers told them, it'll soon be over. Sinethis is drinking from the sky and then the sun will return. It always does.* But when the young were asleep the mothers pulled the remaining dry bedding from the high chambers, and barricaded the entrances. They watched the dyke-water claim the lower levels, and they hoped for the deluge to end.

Whispers sprang up across the marsh. Sinethis, the Great River, was coming, they said. The Folk would bear the price of her thirst. The old stories—children's tales to teach respect for the Great River—passed from mouth to mouth. They told of the Rising, when Sinethis had come to the marsh, driving enemies before her. She had surged in burrows and over-topped banks. She had sung a terrible song of flooding, and of drowning. She had given the Wetted Land its name. And as the River Singers eyed the brimming dykes they felt the truth of the tales. They left their feeding sign as they should, and muttered their prayers. *I offer myself as sacrifice. May your waters be kind.*

They watched. The waters rose. And still the rains came.

PART 1
THE WETTED LAND

'This,' said Strife loudly, as she followed her sister through the tunnels, 'is just typical, isn't it? Just as we're old enough to be out on our own, Mother limits us to mornings and evenings. Don't you think it's typical? I do.'

Ivy ignored her. Kale, walking behind, also said nothing. But in his case that was not unusual.

'I mean,' Strife continued, 'I know Mother doesn't want us out in the middle of the day, what with the rain and everything, but it's not like we're pups any more, is it? I'm sure I could cope with a bit of drizzle now and again.'

Lost in the unfairness of it all, Strife walked heavily into Ivy, who had stopped outside of Uncle Fodur's chambers.

'Ooh, sorry.' Strife backed quickly away, managing to tread on her sister's tail in the process.

'Ouch.' Ivy cradled her tail to her chest, inspecting it for damage. Then she turned to face Strife with an irritated expression. 'Really, Strife. Why can't you stop talking and look where you're going for a change?'

Ivy turned away. Strife pulled a face behind her back.

'And don't pull faces at me,' said Ivy, without looking around.

Strife stuck her tongue out. If her sister was going to be a pain then Strife wasn't going to be grown up about it.

'Uncle Fodur,' called Ivy. 'Are you there?'

'Of course he's there,' said Strife. 'Where else would he be? You know he doesn't like going out.'

'I'm just being polite,' returned

Ivy. 'Something that you seem to find extremely difficult.'

Sometimes the urge to bite her—just once—was overwhelming. Especially now. None of them was in a good mood. Everything in the burrow was damp, including their nest chamber. Even if they could go out, which they couldn't, they would just come back wetter. But at least, thought Strife, they'd be wet and free. Oh, she knew the reasons. It wasn't safe for young voles in the daytime, and enemies were everywhere. Their mother said that she had enough trouble trying to keep up the boundary markers without worrying about whether her children would return alive. And so Strife was stuck with Ivy and Kale. She sighed and put aside the urge to bite her sister. She concentrated instead on waiting for Uncle Fodur. This close to his chambers the smell of rat was strong. Not horrible, but odd, even to Strife who had known him her whole life. It was close to a Singer's smell, but with that sharp note that was never quite right.

'What is it that disturbs me?' came a gruff voice. 'I's a busy rat. Many things to do. No time for puplings. Best you be gone. Not wanted here.'

Strife smiled. This was Fodur's favourite game.

'Oh, come off it,' called Strife. 'You knew we were coming. Mother told us to come and see you. But we're not to be too long this time.'

'Did she, heh? Certain, is you, she not say to keep away

from old Fodur? Knows he eats little Singers does you? Gnaws on their bones?'

Strife giggled. 'You wouldn't eat Singers. You're the softest rat around.'

'Is I indeed? But mayhaps you only sees me when I's not hungry. And today I's a ravening rat. So dares you enter the lair of the great, vicious—'

'Yes we do.' Strife interrupted. 'And you said all that yesterday.'

'Did I?' There came the sound of Fodur chuckling to himself. 'Ack, well. I tries. Best you come in then.'

The young water voles bundled
in. Strife, of course, went first, barging
past Ivy and hurling herself at Fodur—who
gently prised himself free of her embrace and
beamed at the young water voles.

'So, you comes for the stories, does you?'

'Yes, Uncle Fodur,' said Ivy.

'Reminds Fodur: where has we come to in tale, now?'

'Ooh, I can tell you,' said Strife. 'You were drowning,
and Mother and Uncle Sylvan were coming to get you,
and you couldn't swim and the rats had bitten you,
and you were going under the water and—'

'Ah. Heh. I remembers now. Thanks you, Missy
Strife. Mayhaps, now, the rat be speaking, though?'

'That's right, Strife,'
Ivy chipped in.
'You should let
Uncle Fodur
tell it.'

Strife favoured her sister with her most poisonous look.

'I'm sorry,' she said, making sure that Fodur knew that the apology was only for him.

'Not a worry. Now settle and we shall see what is coming.'

Strife plonked herself down next to Kale, against a gnarled iris root. She eyed the root hungrily. In a Singer's burrow it wouldn't have lasted a day. Fodur, though, didn't really eat roots and took a dim view of Folk chewing the walls of his chamber, so Strife forced herself to ignore it. Ivy sat gingerly on Kale's other side, trying to find a dry patch in the soft peat wall. When they were ready, Fodur gave them an approving nod.

'Right. Let's see where we is being. Ah . . . So, waters is lapping at Fodur's head. Your Sinethis, methinks, has her eye on Fodur's life . . . '

Uncle Fodur had a way of telling stories. They were so much better than the old Singer tales, which mainly seemed to be about the horrible things that happened if the Great River was angry or you went near somebody else's territory. Uncle Fodur's stories were different. His had actually happened, for a start: Mother, Uncle Sylvan, and he had come to the Wetted Land from the Great River, and fought the minks and won, and found a home here. Mother never really spoke about it, but Uncle Fodur said that proper stories were the rat way, and a rat who didn't know his history was no rat at all.

And Strife loved to hear them. Despite her hunger, she hardly noticed the afternoon sliding towards a greyish evening. She did not hear her mother's approach until she was outside Fodur's chambers.

'You know, I'm sure that I had some children around here,' their mother said. 'But if I did then surely I should be able to find at least one of them in my burrow when I get home.'

Fodur winked at the pups. 'Time to be going, methinks.'

He ushered them to their feet as their mother pattered in. She smiled at Fodur and ran an amused eye over her offspring.

'Oh, *there* they are. How silly of me. I should have thought to look here. Mainly because they always seem to be here when they're meant to be somewhere else. Like outside, feeding, for example.' She put her head on the side. 'It's evening, you know.'

'Uncle Fodur was telling us about Uncle Sylvan and the fox and Auntie Fern and . . . '

'Yes. Thank you, Strife,' said their mother quickly. 'I thought I told you lot not to be too long? I hope you haven't been taking up too much of Fodur's time?'

'They's always welcome, Miss Aven,' said Fodur.

Their mother smiled. 'Yes, of course. But it's time for their final feed before bed.'

Strife got excitedly to her feet, eyes fixed on the exit from the chamber. Their mother stepped nimbly in front of her.

'First, the rules.'

'But Mother, I—' began Strife.

Their mother cleared her throat. 'Surely you're not going to argue?' she said sweetly.

Strife dropped her gaze. 'No, Mother.'

'Wise choice. Now, what are the rules?'

'Feed quickly, be watchful, keep close to water,' said Strife.

'And?'

'Stay close to the burrow,' said Strife resignedly.

'Correct. Is there any chance that you might actually do that?'

Ivy snorted.

'I will too,' said Strife. 'I'll be just outside. Like Mother says.'

Their mother turned a sceptical eye to her daughter. 'Of course you will. Just as a precaution, though, Kale, if you do see her wandering off could you do me a favour and try to stop her being eaten by a heron or something?'

Kale nodded curtly. 'OK.'

'I don't need him to look after me,' said Strife.

'It's the heron I was worried about,' said their mother with a smile. 'But please remember that there are enemies out there. Be careful.'

'Yes, Mother.'

Their mother surveyed her offspring approvingly. 'What good voles you all are. Off you go, then.'

And Strife, all thought of stories forgotten, scampered joyfully for the burrow entrance. Their mother's final word, shouted after her, went completely unheard in the excitement.

'Carefully!'

As twilight approached the rain eased to a light drizzle. For an instant the clouds broke apart, revealing a bashful sun. Light shone green-gold through a leaf and brought a momentary warmth. But then it faded, leaving only the drizzle. Sylvan smiled ruefully. Oh well. The sun had been nice while it lasted. He eased his way through an overhanging fringe of canary grass, causing water to run from the leaves. It splashed down onto his head and he shook it away, irritably. Frankly, he would be grateful for some dry weather. Then he pulled his attention back to where he was going. He needed to be careful. He was deep inside an unfamiliar territory, and he didn't want to startle the owner. He followed a run down through the plants at the dyke edge, keeping a wary eye out for the resident female.

Despite Sylvan's vigilance she found him before he found her. Half hidden behind a stand of rushes, she had frozen to stillness at the sound of his approach. He did not see her until she jumped across his path, squeaking a challenge. Startled, he leapt up to his haunches, paws raised. The two water voles eyed each other distrustfully.

'What do you want?' the female demanded.

The tone was not quite hostile. Sylvan supposed he should be grateful for that. Females defended their property with sharp words and sharper teeth. The words he could deal with, but he didn't want to be on the receiving end of the rest. During his travels he had met countless Singers. The males were generally all right. They could be avoided or made to leave you alone. The females, though, were another matter, especially if they had young to protect. He hoped fervently that this one didn't. Nesting females were never reasonable. About anything.

'My name's Sylvan,' he said. 'I don't want to cause a problem. I'm just passing through. It's a lovely territory you have here.'

'I'm Mistress Mallow. I know it's lovely. It's mine.' She glared at him. 'Where are you going?'

'Just through, with your permission, Mistress.'

Sylvan risked sinking back to all fours. Mistress Mallow did the same, slowly. A good sign. She pattered a little way forwards and looked him up and down. Then she pulled a face. She didn't seem particularly impressed, and Sylvan couldn't blame her. He had been travelling for a long time and was probably a bit of a state. Nevertheless he felt a flash of irritation. It wasn't as though wanted to be here. He had left behind a comfortable burrow for this, and given the choice he wouldn't have come. But he hadn't had a choice. *She* hadn't given him one.

Sinethis, the Great River, had returned to him with the rain. As the first drops fell into the dyke outside his burrow, her once-familiar song had risen in his mind. It was troubled, fragmented, and discordant, but unmistakably hers. She had pulled him from his home and driven him out into the Wetted Land. And ever since then he had travelled. He had passed alder woods, and fields of reeds; places where the ground was a woven mat of earth and roots, floating above black water, and others where the peat was solid and topped with high tussocks. He had seen the dry edge of the marsh where the dykes ended and grasses rose up to a distant hilltop. The Wetted Land was wide and varied, and only the dykes were constant; running through the heart of the marsh, connecting one to the next to the next, carrying sluggish water to the Great River. And at the dyke edges lived the Singers. These long, thin strips of bank were their home, and their refuge from danger.

For Sylvan the balance was fine. The woods and fields were stuffed with enemies: weasels, stoats, herons. The dyke edges were full of Singers, none of whom were pleased to

see him. And so Sylvan threaded his way between them, running quickly, sleeping in bare grasses, avoiding trouble. Tonight, though, things would be different. He would have a warm nest in a proper burrow. Tonight, Sinethis willing, he would see his sister again. But between him and the promised burrow stood this female. And she was trying to decide whether or not to attack.

Sylvan tried a winning grin. He was probably too bedraggled for it to look convincing, but at least it might persuade her that he was harmless. The female put her head on the side and a half smile played across her lips.

'So. Apparently you're passing through.' Her voice had lost some of its shrillness, replaced by a faint amusement. 'But I want to know *why* you're passing through. Where are you going?'

'To the next territory, Mistress,' said Sylvan, choosing his words carefully. 'I know the female there.'

'Oh yes? What's her name?'

Sylvan battled the temptation to tell her to mind her own

business. *Always be polite to territory owners. Remember their teeth.*

'Mistress Aven, if she still lives there.'

'Ah.' She gave him a knowing look. 'So you're going to see *her* are you? Well good luck to you.'

Sylvan blinked. 'Sorry, what do you mean?'

Now she was definitely amused. 'Oh, nothing, really. I suppose you've met her children, though?'

Aven had children? He really had been away a long time.

'No, I haven't,' he said. 'But I'm looking forward to it.'

'Looking forward to it, you say?' Mistress Mallow chuckled. 'And you a male.'

'Erm, yes. Last time I checked. Why?'

'Never mind. I'm sure it will all be fine,' said Mistress Mallow, who seemed to be enjoying herself. 'They're only children, after all.'

Sylvan was bewildered. 'Just to be clear, these are pups you're talking about?'

Mistress Mallow nodded.

'And you think that they're going give me trouble?'

'Oh, yes.' She smiled. 'They're usually out feeding at about this time, so you'll probably meet them quite soon.'

Sylvan shook his head. He would never understand females. How much bother could Aven's pups possibly be? He glanced up at the clouds. They had fused once more into an ominous grey mass.

'Look, it's lovely to meet you,' said Sylvan, 'and I don't want to seem rude, but I think that I'd better be moving. It's going to be dark soon.'

Mistress Mallow nodded once. 'Of course. I'll show you the way.'

She set off along the bank and he followed obediently. There was no way she would let him further without an escort. She led him down the territory, moving on neat runs that twisted through the bankside plants, and deeper into her home. Stands of reeds and canary grass, and thick layers of herbs towered above him, springing from good, high banks. He nodded at them approvingly. This was a nice place, and it was good to be under proper cover. Deep in the plants with the dyke at his side a Singer could be in the water and away before an enemy had a chance. As long as he heard it, of course.

Eventually Mistress Mallow came to a stop in front of a gigantic boundary marker. The pile of feeding sign and droppings was three times the size of the usual, and perched high above the water level. It was obviously well maintained, and even Sylvan's nose could detect that it was heavily laden with Aven's scent. Sylvan suppressed a smile.

'Well, here you are,' said Mistress Mallow. 'This is the edge of my territory.'

'I don't think I could miss it.'

'Yes,' she said sourly. 'I'm sure that's the idea.'

Sylvan took in the expanse of grasses and iris before him. The dyke was wider here, and deep. The far side was a mix of reeds and great sedges, and the trees were further from the dyke edge. A Singer's paradise. Aven was doing well.

'Looks like she's been expanding.'

'She tries.'

'Oh, sorry,' said Sylvan, remembering who he was talking to. 'Anyway, thanks for showing me the way. It was good of you.'

'A pleasure,' said Mistress Mallow. 'It's always nice to come down here and see how much territory I've lost.'

Sylvan grinned. 'I'm sure you hold your own.'

Mistress Mallow looked quite pleased at that. Sylvan thanked her again and stepped over the boundary marker. Then he eased his way through the dripping plants and into Aven's territory. 'Good luck with the children,' she called after him.

Strife and Kale munched in happy silence, side by side in Strife's favourite eating spot. She had found it on one of her first outings. She liked it because both purple and yellow loosestrife grew from the banks here. Also it was excitingly close to the trees, the border of Mistress Mallow's territory, and the world beyond. She was not old enough, yet, but soon she would go out and find her own place. She would have a territory as full of loosestrife as possible. She liked the flowers mainly because she was named after them. Kale didn't seem to have much of an opinion about either the loosestrife or the patch, but then he rarely put enough words together to voice an opinion on anything. But Strife suspected that he would come here even if Mother didn't ask him to. It was some sort of weird brother thing. And, of course, the fact that it got him away from Ivy probably helped. Under extreme duress Strife might admit that her sister was generally OK. But Ivy had a nasty habit of doing what Mother said. And Strife considered Ivy's refusal to venture further than the burrow entrance nothing short of contemptibly boring. She sometimes wondered if they were really from the same litter, or if Ivy had accidentally been left with them by a field vole.

The rain fell softly onto the leaves around her. It made quite a nice noise, like a constant whisper. Despite the wet it felt good to be out. Strife dropped the remnants of the young iris shoot she had been eating onto her pile of feeding sign. She scratched, luxuriously, then grabbed for a loosestrife stem and chewed it to pieces. They would have to go back before it was dark—even she wouldn't try their mother's limits too far—but there was still time to stock up.

18

'You're quiet,' observed Kale, dropping more grass onto his pile.

'And you're a fine one to talk,' she said with her mouth full. She swallowed. 'Not that you do, much.'

Kale shrugged and took another bite of his grass.

'But for your information I don't *have* to be speaking the whole time,' said Strife. 'I'm perfectly able to be quiet if I want to. It's just that I like to give everyone the benefit of my opinion when something important occurs to me.'

Strife took a large bite of iris. From somewhere down near Mistress Mallow's territory a Singer called out. Strife could barely make it out over the drizzle, but it sounded like a male's voice. She stopped chewing. The Singer called again, still distant but louder. There was something about it—an urgency. Next to her Kale's head came up. She quietly placed her iris on the ground, listening intently. Nothing. No sign that anything was out of the ordinary. Even so, her heart began to thump.

'What is it?' she whispered.

Kale shook his head, gazing out through the vegetation. Birds still sang overhead. No attack from above, then. Safe to look. Kale, as if reading her thoughts, rose up onto his hind legs and scented the air. He frowned and sniffed again. Then he went utterly still. Not even a whisker twitched. He dropped with the utmost care to all fours.

'Strife.' Kale spoke softly, urgently. 'Don't move.'

'Why?' she hissed. 'What is it?'

Then she caught it. The wind changed and a small breeze swirled into the feeding patch. It brought with it a tendril of scent, foul in her nostrils, heavy and sharp and sickly. Stoat. Oh, please not a stoat. Powerful jaws, reed-thin and muscular: quick death for the unwary. And they hadn't heard it. And it was close: close enough to smell.

'Be ready,' said Kale.

Be ready. She glanced over at the dyke edge. She had thought they were feeding right next to the water. That's what Mother told them to do. But they had wandered deep into the patch. The water was beyond jumping distance; only a dash away, but now that was horribly far. Her legs began to shake. She tried to still them but they would not obey. Oh, why hadn't she been more careful? Stop it. No time for that. Focus. They would have one chance. That's how stoats were. Move too soon or too slowly, or jump the wrong way, and they would take you. Wait for the rustle, until its scent fills your nostrils. Choose. Run. Dive for the water. Then you might live. Strife tensed.

The strange male Singer's voice called out again. It was louder this time. She caught the word. *Stoat*. It sounded like he was trying to warn them. Why would he do that? With the voice came the distant sound of plants being thrust aside and feet splashing through shallows. That was ridiculous. He was running towards them. Maybe he's stoat-proof, she thought hysterically. She almost laughed, but swallowed it. A sound would be fatal. The crashing noises from the running Singer grew louder.

The stoat too heard the noises. From the grasses, the merest fraction from where they stood, it rose up: a monster made of fur and teeth. It gazed away at the source of the sounds. Strife could clearly see the white pelt of its chest rise as it breathed in the scents. It hesitated, swaying on the spot. A loud crash from the Singer. The stoat's head whipped further around, seeking its prey—

—and Strife hurled herself at the dyke, smashing though plants and leaping for the water. Kale split the surface next to her and together they knifed down into the cool depths.

They swam side by side through the water plants, twisting along the length of the dyke to where the stoat could not follow. When they had swum far enough they surfaced and hauled out on the opposite bank. Strife turned to face the spot where—until a moment before—they had been feeding. Two black stoat's eyes peered at her through the fresh hole in the screen of canary grass. From further along the dyke the sound of the strange male's progress was clear. He was going to run straight into the stoat. Strife opened her mouth to shout, but too late. The male crashed into view. The stoat wheeled, lunged, snapped. The male leapt. For an instant she thought that the stoat had him. But then the Singer vanished into the water with a plop. The stoat was left alone on the bank. It sniffed about it, seeking its lost prey. It snaked back and forth across the feeding place. And then, with a hiss, it whipped away and was gone.

Calm descended. The birds sang overhead, heedless of the drama below. Patches of duckweed, floating on the dyke surface, bobbed on the ripples and went still. Raindrops puckered the water. A stream of bubbles rose up and popped. And then a large River Singer's face thrust up through the water close to where they stood. He scrabbled for an instant at the slippery bank before pulling himself out. He glanced over at the far bank, long enough to register the stoat's absence. Then he turned to face Strife and Kale.

'Well,' he said cheerfully. 'That could have been nasty, couldn't it?'

Sylvan regarded the two young voles in front of him. They stared, wide-eyed and unspeaking. *They might be in shock*, he thought. First stoat and everything. He tried again, trying to sound sympathetic.

'Are you both OK?'

Nothing. Not even a blink. Poor things.

'Look, I know it's scary, but that stoat was just trying its luck. It couldn't really hope to take you once you knew it was there. I followed its scent down the bank. Mistress Mallow told me that you might be out feeding, so I called to warn you. Just in case.'

The small female and the male exchanged glances. The male nodded, almost imperceptibly. Then the female said, 'You're covered with weed.'

He glanced at the water. Where he had hauled out, the duckweed had a vole-sized hole in it.

'I'm sure it's very fetching.'

'Pretty silly, actually.'

Sylvan groomed some of the weed off. 'Nothing new there. It seems to be my permanent state.'

'Are you going to eat us?' asked the female, conversationally.

'*What?*'

'Mother says not to talk to strange males because they might eat us.'

Sylvan couldn't quite believe a mother would tell that to a pup. 'Really?'

'Yes.'

'Strange. Anyway, I'm not going to eat you.' He smiled. 'You're too hairy for a start.'

'I'd stick in your throat,' said the female, almost proudly. Then she nodded at her brother. 'He'd poison you. My name's Lou. It's short for Loosestrife.'

Her brother made a snorting sound. 'Her name's Strife.'

The female rounded on him. 'You didn't have to say that.

Why'd you say that? I've never had anyone to call me Lou. It's always Strife this and Strife that, and this was my first chance to meet somebody who might call me Lou, and you've ruined it for me. You always ruin everything, Kale, I . . . '

The tirade continued. Sylvan watched with a kind of horrified fascination as the words poured out of her. Her brother bore the verbal assault with quiet stoicism. He had obviously learned to wait it out.

'I tell you what,' said Sylvan when Strife seemed to be nearly finished. 'I'll call you Lou, if you'd like.'

For some reason this did not have the desired effect. The female gave him a suspicious look. 'No. You call me Strife like everybody else.'

Strife, thought Sylvan. *Seems about right.*

'Whatever you say,' he said.

'I don't trust you. Mother says not to trust adults who are nice to us.'

'No she doesn't,' said Kale. 'You made that up.'

'I—' began Strife.

'Look,' said Sylvan, cutting her off before she could begin again, 'I've come here to see your Mother. Is she around?'

'No,' said Kale blandly.

'Not on your nelly,' added Strife, looking smug.

Sylvan blinked. What was wrong with these voles?

'Any particular reason?'

'Mother doesn't want any strange males around.'

'I'm not a strange male.'

'Yes you are,' said Kale.

'You look pretty strange to me,' said Strife. 'You're covered with duckweed. That's not normal.'

Sylvan could feel his temper fraying. Talking to these two was like smacking his head against a tree root.

'If you hadn't noticed,' he said, 'I've just stopped you from being eaten by a stoat. Doesn't that count for anything?'

Kale shrugged.

'Not really,' said Strife.

'Well, there's gratitude for you. I can certainly tell that you're Aven's children.'

A slight hesitation. Then Strife said, 'Aven? Who's Aven?' She gave him what was apparently her best attempt at an innocent look.

Kale frowned. 'You know Mother?'

'No,' said Sylvan sarcastically. 'I'm just really good at guessing names.'

'Proves nothing,' Strife hissed—very audibly—to Kale, who nodded. The pair of them squared up so that they blocked Sylvan's path.

Sylvan looked helplessly from one exasperating vole to the other. Then his jaw set. There was no way he was going to have hiked halfway across the marsh and be stopped by a couple of pups.

'Oh, well,' he said. 'I suppose that if your minds are made up then I'd best be going.'

Sylvan turned as if to set off. Then he dodged past them and sprinted up the bank. He ducked under a spray of sweet-grass and dashed back down to the water's edge. He permitted himself a brief smugness at Strife's outraged squeak, and then bustled off deeper into Aven's territory. After a moment there was a rustle and Strife and Kale fell in behind him, jogging to keep up.

'You're going completely the wrong way you know,' called Strife. Sylvan did not reply. 'Wrong, wrong, wrong,' she continued, 'couldn't be more wrong if you tried. Mother's nest is nowhere near here. If only you knew how wrong you are . . . '

Sylvan put his head down, concentrating on where he

was going. He tried to ignore the stream of unhelpful advice from Strife, but there was a quality to her voice that was almost impossible to shut out. As he walked she chattered blithely behind him about how other males had been here before and come this way, and they had all been wrong, you know, and they hadn't listened to the wise young River Singers and one of them taken a bad turn and got eaten by a badger, if badgers eat Singers, which she didn't know if they did, but if they *did* then that probably must have happened, and it really wasn't all that good for them, you know?

Sylvan did his best, but eventually he could take no more. He stopped dead, eyes closed. He took a calming breath and then turned to face Strife.

'Is there any chance,' he said, 'that you could stop talking for a moment?'

Strife considered this, head on one side. 'Not really,' she concluded. 'I mean, I meant everything I said about those males and one of them . . . '

Sylvan walked up to Strife until they were almost nose to nose. Her babble trailed off as he approached. She blinked at him, innocently.

'Please,' he said. 'I've had a really long day and we were just attacked by a stoat. I need some quiet. I mean, don't you have to breathe or something?'

Behind him something parted the grasses.

'What's going on out here?' a voice demanded. 'And what in the name of Sinethis is this male doing here?'

Sylvan turned. Then he grinned at his sister's shocked expression.

'Hello, Aven,' he said—and was knocked to the ground as Aven flung herself at him, squeaking with delight. For an instant he wondered if he was being greeted or attacked. But then Aven, apparently remembering that her children were watching, climbed off him. She stood up and touched her nose to his, still grinning.

'So,' she said. 'You came back, then. And about time, too.' She glanced up at the sky. 'It'll be dark soon, so let's get you to the burrow.'

Their mother set off, moving swiftly back to the main entrance. The strange male fell in behind her. Strife caught Kale's eye, wondering what on earth was going on. He looked as mystified as she was. He gestured after their mother with his chin. *Better follow*, the gesture said, *or we'll never find out*.

'Good point,' said Strife.

She scampered after the male's retreating back. It always seemed to be this way with adults, she reflected. Just as you were getting a grip on how things should be they went and completely changed the rules. All of her life one thing had been absolute: no strange males were allowed near the main burrow. That probably would have gone for females too, if there were any who were stupid enough to trespass on their mother's patch. The reason, which Strife thought was very silly indeed, was Uncle Fodur. Uncle Fodur was . . . well, he was Uncle Fodur. But he was also a rat. What difference that might make to anyone was beyond her. Fodur had tried to explain it once. It was all right, he said, when it was just one rat and one Singer. Or even a few and a few. But many rats and many Singers all trying to live in the same place would end up fighting for the same burrows. Strife had pointed out that Uncle Fodur used almost the same burrow as she did and she wasn't trying to bite him, now, was she? Uncle Fodur chuckled. It's different in a family, he said. That, at least, made some sort of sense.

In any case Strife took great pride in her work. The average male never got close before she made him regret the day he was born; or, more accurately, the day that *she* was born. She could irritate anyone into submission. And now here *she* was following an unfamiliar male who their mother had just invited in. Something weird was happening.

Their mother stopped on the bank opposite the burrow entrance. She checked for predators then slid into the water and paddled across. The male followed, swimming strongly. Strife stared after him.

'Who do you think he is?' Strife asked as Kale pulled alongside.

Kale shrugged and slipped into the dyke.

'Where's your curiosity?' Strife called after him. Then she cast herself into the water and swam until her paws connected with the knot of submerged roots in the burrow entrance.

She scrambled over them and up into the relative dryness of the burrow. She shook the water from her fur and headed up to the main chamber where a collection of wet River Singers was waiting for her. Only Ivy, who had obviously been in for ages, was relatively dry.

'Well, here we are, then,' said her mother. She gestured around the main chamber. 'Home damp home.'

The male nodded approvingly. 'It's a great place, Tiny.'

Strife goggled. Any Singer commenting on their mother's size would normally expect to go home carrying their nose in their paws.

'What have I told you about calling me that?' said her mother.

'You said not to do it, because you'd hurt me.'

'Right.'

Strife couldn't begin to imagine how he was getting away with it. Not only was he still alive, but their mother didn't even seem to be too offended.

'Anyway,' said their mother, 'wait here, I've got a surprise for you.'

Their mother pattered away down a side tunnel, leaving her children alone with the strange male. Questions needed answering. Strife plonked herself down in front of him and gave him one of her best and most searching stares. After a few moments he began to look uncomfortable.

'Yes, hello?'

'You called Mother "Tiny". Don't you mind pain?'

He smiled. 'Don't worry. I'll live.'

She never got a chance to begin the interrogation. From the side tunnel came the familiar sound of Uncle Fodur, huffing his way down towards them. He limped down into the chamber, bad leg clutched beneath his body. He was out of breath, Strife thought. He must have run here from his nest. When his gaze fell on the male a delighted smile spread across his face.

'Is you!' Fodur cried. 'You comes back.'

'Fodur!' The male stood in shock for an instant and then ran forwards. They touched noses and then the male put a paw on Uncle Fodur's shoulder. Both of them were grinning stupidly.

'I thought you had your own burrow?' said the male.

'Ah. Heh. That not be working out too well. So I lives here, thanks to Missy Aven.'

'Excuse me,' said Strife. 'You know Uncle Fodur?'

'Fodur? Of course I do. He's the best rat in the marsh.'

Fodur winked. 'Only rat too. But I's being a rude rat. Puplings,' he said, turning to Kale, Ivy and Strife, 'this is your Uncle Sylvan.' He put his head on the side. 'But you has met, methinks.'

'Yes,' said Sylvan giving Strife a wry look. 'You could say that.'

Strife's ears went hot. He was *Sylvan*. The one from the story. The one who had saved Uncle Fodur from drowning and brought their mother to the Wetted Land, who had fought with a mink and lived. And she had been irritating him. She wanted to curl into her fur. But Sylvan was not paying any attention.

'It's great to see you, Fodur.'

'Same to be seeing you. But am curious why you's back?'

'Oh,' said Sylvan. 'I have my reasons. But maybe I'd better tell you later on.' As he said it his gaze took in Strife and Kale. Fodur and her mother nodded knowingly. Their faces clearly said that whatever the reasons were, the 'children' would almost certainly not get to hear about them. And that, Strife decided, was entirely unacceptable. She forgot instantly about her embarrassment. Something interesting was happening and if she wasn't careful she'd never find out what.

'Excuse me, Mother,' she said with her politest voice.

'Yes, dear?'

'I'm quite tired. Would it be all right if I went up to the nest for a sleep?'

Their mother's eyes narrowed. Strife met her gaze with an expression of complete guilelessness. She considered throwing in a yawn for good measure.

Their mother shook her head in bewilderment. 'Fine. If you want to go for a sleep I can't see any problem.'

'Can Kale and Ivy come too?'

'If they want.'

'But—' began Ivy.

'Come on,' said Strife, shoving at Ivy's rear with both paws. 'It's time for all good voles to go to bed. I'm sure you wouldn't want Sylvan to think you're badly behaved, would you?'

And with that Strife chivvied her perplexed siblings out of the main chamber and escorted them firmly up the tunnel towards their nest.

'We shouldn't do this,' whispered Kale. 'It's private.'

'Shush. I'm concentrating,' said Strife. 'I want to hear what they're saying.'

'Because you like Sylvan.'

'Oh, grow up,' she said. 'I'm after information, that's all.'

They had left Ivy, of course, back in the nest chamber. She would not approve of this. Normally they were not allowed here on their own. It was right under the upper feeding hole and not really safe. But an intrigued Strife was never going to sit quietly while the grown-ups discussed important things

without her. So she continued her search, creeping across the tiny hollow, one ear to the ground. It was definitely somewhere around here. The scant twilight filtering from the feeding hole was barely enough to see by. But Strife only needed her ears for this. She had spent ages furtively excavating a place just off one of the disused tunnels, in a dark corner behind a large knot of grass roots. She was fairly certain that her mother didn't know about it and fervently

hoped she would never find out. In the right place the floor was thin enough to hear nearly everything that was said in the main chamber below. It was a risk, certainly, but it had been extremely useful in the past. Having advanced warning was, in Strife's opinion, a lot better than sticking around to get told off. Ah. There we go. The perfect spot.

'. . . sorry about the children. I hope they didn't give you too much bother.' Their mother's voice.

'Nothing I couldn't handle,' said Sylvan.

'Huh. That's what he thinks,' muttered Strife. Kale gave her a curious look and then hunkered down next to her, ear to the floor.

'Thought you said it was private,' Strife whispered.

Kale's expression said *oh well.*

'. . . did a pretty good job of keeping me out, though,' Sylvan continued. 'I guess that's a good idea, given Fodur.'

'Is true. I's much too dangerous for other Singers.'

'Only if Aven found them bullying you.'

Fodur chuckled. 'Is right, that.'

'Well,' said their mother. 'The main trick is to stop anyone from finding out he's here. Thankfully the only thing my daughter enjoys more than talking is getting in people's way.'

Strife nearly squeaked with indignation. Only her desire to hear what Sylvan had to say prevented her from marching down and demanding an apology.

'Anyway,' continued their mother. 'Have you seen our brother, recently?'

'Orris?' said Sylvan. 'Actually I was with him a couple of days ago.'

'Really? How is he?'

Sylvan gave a short laugh. 'Fat, mainly. I suppose that means he's happy. Difficult to tell with Orris. He's found himself a nice place with deep banks and huge tussocks.'

'That'll please him,' said their mother. 'He's never really been one for the water.'

'True. He said this way he'd be able to escape enemies without having to swim.'

'Sensible Singer, methinks,' said Fodur. 'Your Sinethis is too wet to be fooling with.'

A short silence.

'You know, you have a point there, Fodur,' said Sylvan. 'About Sinethis. But I never have the option of leaving her be.

River Singers are children of the Great River. Even here, it seems.'

Strife frowned in the darkness. All pups knew about Sinethis. *We are River Singers, children of the Great River, she shelters us*, and that sort of thing. But Sylvan was speaking about her as if she really existed.

'You has your mind on things, methinks,' said Fodur.

'It's that easy to spot, is it?'

'No, but I's no ordinary rat. I's perceptive.'

'I might have known,' said their mother. 'It's too much to hope that you'd visit and we could just have a chat and feed together.' She had an odd tone, as if she was not really joking. 'So what is it?'

A pause.

'It's complicated. It has to do with the Great River.'

'Doesn't everything? What about her?'

Sylvan hesitated. 'She's started calling to me again. That's what.'

Next to Strife, Kale tensed. She glanced over at him. His whiskers had gone stiff with shock.

'What's wrong?' she whispered.

Kale shook his head and held up a forestalling paw. He wanted to listen.

' . . . mean calling to you again,' their mother was saying. 'I don't understand.'

'I. That is . . . well, I never really told you.' Sylvan sounded awkward. 'I mean while we were running from the mink there was too much happening and afterwards, well, Sinethis went away and I thought that it was over. And we had to set up our homes here and everything, so I never really got around to it.'

'Sylvan,' said their mother, 'is there any chance you could tell me what you're blithering about?'

'Sorry. I haven't tried to explain this before. Look, back when we were children I started hearing Sinethis. Just before Mother was taken. It was like she flowed into my head and spoke to me. She told me things. She guided me to the Wetted Land. She's the reason we're here.'

Next to Strife, Kale shifted again. He moved his head to the side as if he were trying to shake the words free from it. His breathing was loud in the tiny space.

'That's the most ridiculous thing I've ever heard,' said their mother.

'No,' said Sylvan, speaking more firmly. 'It's not ridiculous. It happened, Aven. I heard Sinethis. She guided us here and then she left me. And now she's back. There's something coming. I think she's trying to warn me.'

'Oh, come on, Sylvan—' began their mother, but Fodur interrupted.

'Not meaning to be speaking out of turn, but methinks is best you hear. If Sinethis speak to Sylvan mayhaps she has reasons.'

Strife felt the fur at her neck begin to prick upright. She glanced at Kale. He was now completely still, eyes closed. His chest was heaving.

'Kale,' hissed Strife. 'What is it?'

Kale shook his head, eyes shut tight.

'Kale, you're scaring me. What's wrong?'

'I'm sorry, Aven,' said Sylvan below them. 'I came here to warn you. And I will go in the morning. Before it's too late.'

'Sylvan, stop it.' said their mother, below. 'Listen to yourself. Warn me about what? Before *what's* too late? This doesn't make sense.'

'It does make sense,' Sylvan insisted. 'Sinethis came to me with the rain. She sounds different but it's her. She's calling and I have to follow. I'm going back to the Great River.'

'Why?' Their mother's voice was small, now. Almost scared.

'The Rising,' said Sylvan.

Kale's eyes snapped open. He gasped. He pawed at his whiskers in distress. Strife had no time to react before he scrambled around and dashed from the chamber. She made a belated grab for him, but caught only the tip of his tail which whipped through her paws and was gone. It happened in an instant. She sat in shock as the sound of Kale's paws skittered away down the tunnels. She should follow him. He might need her help. But then another snatch of conversation drifted up to her.

' . . . the way Sinethis sounds. She's broken up: kind of distant and angry at the same time. And there's talk all over the marsh.'

'That's just talk.' But Strife heard the uncertainty in her mother's voice.

'Look, I know how it sounds. I can't say anything for sure and I don't know what you can do even if it *is* coming. But I had to warn you.'

'But why the river, Sylvan?' Her mother was almost pleading. 'After everything we lost there. You're not . . . ' her voice trailed off.

'Looking for her?' A pause, then softly, 'No. Fern's dead. She was taken. I know that. But Sinethis is calling me. And I have to go.'

Nobody else spoke. *Right*, thought Strife. *That's enough.* She needed to find Kale. She had never before seen him so much as twitch a whisker in surprise. And now he had run away after hearing a conversation. This was bad and it needed to be sorted out. Strife backed out of the small hollow and into the tunnel. Night noises percolated through the peat walls of the burrow: frogs, crickets, and the occasional splash. The sounds jumbled with the thoughts in her mind. Strife closed her eyes, trying to make sense of it all. The Rising, whatever that was. Fern: that could be Aunt Fern from the stories. She and Sylvan had been attacked by a fox and Sylvan escaped by hurling himself into the Great River. She had been taken. Sinethis speaking sounded stupid. But something about that had made Kale run away. That was the strangest thing of all. Strife opened her eyes. Something serious was happening. And she was going to find out what.

Strife scurried up the trampled earth ramp to the nest chamber she shared with Ivy and Kale. Even in the daytime hardly any light penetrated this deep into the burrow. Now the darkness was absolute. She sniffed the air and listened. The air was warm and damp. The room was thick with Ivy's scent, and Strife could hear her breathing. But Kale's scent was old. He had not been here. Strife pattered in and pawed at her sister's shoulder.

'Ivy. Are you awake?' she whispered.

Ivy was curled up with her back to Strife, buried in soft grasses.

'No,' said Ivy. 'I'm not.'

She clearly had not been asleep. She sounded sulky.

'Ivy, I need your help.'

Ivy rolled over, scrabbling free of the covering grasses.

'Oh you do, do you? And why would I give you my help, exactly?' Ivy hissed.

Strife was taken aback. 'Because I'm your sister.'

'Hah,' said Ivy bitterly. 'Some sister you are. Because of you I had to go to bed early. I never even got a chance to talk to Sylvan. And as soon as we're in the nest, oh, then you and Kale run off together to do something fun. And I'm here on my own; boring old Ivy left out as usual. It's not fair.'

Ivy threw herself back down into the bedding. A horrid feeling welled up in Strife. Kale had run away. And now Ivy was angry with her. It was turning into a mess. But she could make it better. Strife stroked vaguely at the bristling fur on her sister's back.

'Ivy?'

No response.

'Ivy, I'm really sorry. I didn't think. I didn't mean to leave you out. But Kale's gone,' she blurted.

Ivy uncurled a little.

'What do you mean "gone"?'

'I don't know. He was upset and ran away.'

'Why would he do that?'

'I don't know. He heard something he shouldn't have and ran off. And I don't know where he is. I'm frightened for him.'

Ivy sighed. 'Don't be silly, Strife. It's not really a problem. He'll still be in the burrow.'

'But what if he's not?'

'He's not going out at night, is he?' Ivy scoffed. 'All you have to do is look for him.'

'But he was upset,' said Strife. 'It'd be easier with two of us. Oh, won't you help me? Please?'

The darkness around Ivy gave the impression of a vole considering her options.

'You know what? I'm not going to. You two never include me in anything. So you'll have to go on your own.'

Strife was aghast. 'But what if he's hurt or he left the burrow or something?'

'He hasn't,' said Ivy firmly. 'He's not that stupid. Frankly, he's probably just trying to get some peace and quiet away from you for a bit. And I can't say I blame him.'

Strife opened her mouth. Then she shut it again.

Ivy continued, 'And next time you're planning something maybe you'll think of somebody else for a change.'

Then Ivy huddled back down into her nesting material. Strife heard her turn her back and pull the grasses back over her. The sound had an air of finality.

'Right,' whispered Strife. 'Well, thank you very much. I *will* go and look for him. And if he's hurt I hope you're happy with yourself.'

'Go away, Strife.'

'Fine.'

Strife ran from the nest and set off down the tunnels. Angry tears pricked her eyes, but she blinked them away. She didn't need

THE WETTED LAND

Ivy's help. She would find Kale with or without her. From beneath her she could hear the adults, their voices muted by the earth to a low mumble. She would have to keep to the upper levels, and move quietly. She was not doing anything wrong, exactly, but life would definitely be easier if Mother never found out about this. Strife crept along the tunnel to the junction where it forked. She hesitated, scenting the air. One branch was fresher, leading to tunnels that ended at the main entrance. The smells from the other were packed with earthy, warm scents, and a trace of Kale, faint, but recent. She took this fork and followed it as it ran along the dyke edge. As with the nest chamber, these passages were utterly dark, but Strife knew every twist by heart. Her whiskers brushed the walls and floor ahead of her, telling her the shape of the tunnel. Underlying everything was the smell of her mother and siblings, layer upon layer of it. This was their place. Their scent wove through the fabric of the burrow; and over the top of it, a single, new thread of Kale's smell hung in the air, faint but reassuring.

Another junction. Two options: straight on or right. Kale's scent came from the tunnel that led deeper into the bank. She barely paused, her feet carrying her onward. This tunnel, she knew, curved back on itself and dipped down to another set of entrances, less used and lying further towards Mistress Mallow's territory. Strife had often come here as a pup before they were allowed out. It had seemed an adventure, expanding their world in the days before they knew about the marsh. The air around Strife grew cooler, wafting up from the outside, bringing with it a sharper scent of her brother. As she dropped down towards the water the darkness softened to a featureless grey, lit by cloud-muted moonlight. A water vole's haunches made a blacker shape against the tunnel wall. Kale. Thank Sinethis.

Kale froze at the sound of her approach and whirled, squeaking a challenge.

'It's me, you complete idiot,' said Strife.

She came to a stop a little way from him. He was sitting in the passage that ran to the burrow entrance, a little way back from the water. He groomed his whiskers, and regarded her solemnly. She returned his gaze, her head on one side. Neither of them spoke for a long while. Strife gave in first. After all, she thought, if she had to wait for Kale to speak they could be there all night.

'I tell you what,' said Strife, 'let's do this the easy way. I know that you won't want to tell me what's going on. You think that you can keep it to yourself and I'm just going to have to just lump it. Right?'

Kale nodded.

'Thought so. The trouble is that I *really* want to know what's happening and I'm going to be really loud, annoying, and unreasonable about it until you tell me. Are you with me so far?'

A thoughtful look. Then another nod. Good, thought Strife. There was no point having a reputation if you couldn't use it when you needed to.

'So,' she continued, 'I have an idea. Let's assume that I've already been as horrid as I can be for a *very* long time, and that you've finally given in and decided to tell me what I want to know. Then I can help you with whatever's on your mind and we can both go back to the nest and get some sleep.'

Strife watched Kale carefully. He did not even blink.

'So how about it?'

'I'm not going to the nest. I'm going out,' said Kale.

Strife's mouth dropped open. He may as well have said he wanted to be a badger.

'Out? What do you mean out?'

'Out,' said Kale. He pointed with his jaw. 'That way.'

Strife stared past him to the water beyond. Until recently the tunnel had ended at a muddy platform among the reeds. But now the dyke had risen the passage was cut short by a flat expanse of water. It shimmered darkly a little way from where Kale sat. When the platforms had first submerged Strife had invented a method of sprinting down and launching full pelt into the water. The idea was that any heron waiting for a River Singer would get the shock of its life. So far the only thing she had surprised was a moorhen, but she lived in hope. During the day it was fun. But now the sight of the water gave Strife an unhappy feeling, like it could surge up and smother them in blackness.

'That,' said Strife as if talking to an idiot, 'is outside of the burrow.'

Kale nodded.

'At night' she added, just in case he hadn't understood. 'In the dark.'

Kale nodded again.

Strife ran a paw over her eyes. 'Right. I see. If you've been feeling like this why didn't you just let the stoat take you earlier? It'd be easier than wandering around waiting for a fox to eat you.'

'You don't understand.'

'Well, here's an idea, then: why don't you try explaining it to me?'

Kale wrestled with the thought for some moments. Then he shook his head. 'It's personal,' he said.

'Oh, great. Well that's all right then. So when Mother asks me why you decided to end it all I can tell her that it was personal.'

'I'm not asking you to be here.' Kale turned to face the outside world. Somewhere in the trees beyond the dyke a tawny owl called out. He flinched.

'Ooh,' said Strife. 'That was an owl, wasn't it? What is it Mother calls them? "Death on wings" or something? Wouldn't be pleasant being caught by one of those. All those talons are bad for the health.'

Kale said nothing.

'So, are you sure you're still going out? Not going to tell your sister what's going on? Or at least wait until morning?'

Kale lowered his head. 'OK,' he said. 'You're right. Let's go back to the nest.'

Strife nudged Kale's shoulder. 'It's a good thing you had me here to talk to you. At least somebody is being sensible.' She set off back up the tunnel, calling over her shoulder, 'But don't think you're going to get away without telling me what's going on.'

Kale, though, did not answer. Instead, Strife heard a noise she would remember for the rest of her life. It was the sound of a River Singer casting himself into the water, giving himself to Sinethis and paddling into the night. She stopped dead in shock. Then she whirled about and dashed to the entrance. It was empty. Kale was gone.

Strife peered out into the night. She could barely see. Ripples rolled grey on black as they sloshed into the passage, lit by the murky underside of the sky. Apart from the ripples there was no sign of her brother.

'Kale!' she shouted.

Then she shut her mouth and clamped her paws over it. She shouldn't have done that. If any enemy heard a Singer call it would be led straight to her. Or to Kale. But what could she do? She could run to Mother, but that would take time and Kale was swimming away. Even as she thought it, she heard a faint splashing noise and a stir in the plants on the far bank. It could have been a vole climbing from the water. Kale was leaving, and she was dithering. Think, Strife. A ripple lapped the earth at her feet, making a tiny sound. The noise was insignificantly small, but it seemed to somehow flow up from the dyke. It chimed in Strife's thoughts and faded. Strange. She concentrated, seeking the source of the feeling. And before she knew what she was doing, her body slid into the water. Two strong kicks, a pull with the legs, and she was beyond the burrow and swimming in the blackness of the dyke. A rush of cold, a beat of the heart, and Strife came to her senses. Fear poured into her. This was insane. They were out at night. Both of them were going to die. And if she did catch Kale, she thought grimly, she might even kill him herself. She wanted to turn, head home, fetch Mother. But she did not. The choice was made. The water rippled inkily as she swam for the far side. The bank rose up before her, a dark wall of tattered shapes. She felt plants beneath her paws and scrabbled at them, dragging her body up and into the sedges. She huddled on the bankside, cold, wet, and breathing heavily. She looked back across to her home but could not see it. The burrow may as well have been wiped from existence.

Strife cowered, listening to the night sounds. Crickets, a tiny breath of wind through the sedges. Nothing else. It took some moments for her to register the full meaning of that. Oh, no. It was *quiet*. The constant hiss of rain had gone. The drizzle had stopped. The air was dry. That meant that her scent would linger. The sound of her movements would travel. And night birds would be able to hunt. As if in confirmation a tawny owl called out. It was close by, overhead in the trees near to where she sat.

'Oh, Sinethis,' Strife whispered.

She should run for the burrow. This was too dangerous. But she caught a noise from further up the bank: a whisper of grass stems and a small snapping sound. *Kale*, she thought. It had to be. And he was just ahead. But then the owl called again and launched with a crack of twigs and a rattle of leaves. Silence. Strife's gaze snapped up as a dim, grey shape ghosted overhead. It passed, wheeled, and then plunged down into the grasses on the bank ahead of her. A dull thump. A terrified squeak. Kale! Rustles, growing fainter. The owl leapt back into the air, following the sounds of the fleeing Singer. It had missed its target, but now the hunt was on.

Terror surged through Strife. It was hunting Kale. She scrambled to her feet, moving without thinking. She dashed along the bank, making for the source of the noises.

Somewhere a tiny part of her mind was screaming at her to stop, to think, but she shut it out. No time for that. Plants whipped wetly across her muzzle and flung their water in her eyes. She thrust them aside and fled on down the dyke-bank runs. She had a sense of space as she burst into a small clearing. She stopped, instinctively. Listen. Nothing. No sound. She glanced up . . .

. . . and hurled herself to the side. She landed, sprawling, among the sweet-grass and rolled to her feet. She went utterly still. Where, until an instant before, she had been standing, the space was filled with talons. She raised her gaze. White-feathered legs, a powerful body, a cruelly hooked beak, and two black eyes set into a broad, whitish face. The owl straightened. It lifted a claw to examine the ground beneath it. Then the claw flashed down, raking at the plants a fraction from Strife's head. She leapt away, shoving into the grasses behind her. The owl saw the movement. Another claw lashed out.

Strife jumped back as talons dragged at the plants, leaving ruts in the soil in front of her face. She tried to back away, but the grasses behind her meshed, tangled, held firm. She spun to face the net of plants in a desperate attempt to force her way through. But she was trapped. She turned back to face the owl. It leant forward until it was nothing but beak and eyes. It opened its beak. She whimpered.

A squeak and rustle from the plants to the side. The owl was distracted only for an instant but it was all Strife needed. She flung herself past it, clawed her way round the clump of grasses and dived for the dyke. She hit the water badly, flat on the surface, and the impact knocked the breath from her. She gasped and her mouth filled with water. She coughed and thrashed, trying to clear her lungs. Dimly she saw the owl lift up from the grasses, gain height. One more cough. A gasp of air. The owl hovered overhead. Then Strife dived down through the water plants, twisting her way to the dyke floor.

Lost in the silence of the depths, two sets of talons

trailed through the water's surface, grasping for a water vole who was gone.

Strife swam with short, panicked strokes. Her mind raced. The owl was up there, waiting for her to come up. She needed to be where it didn't expect her. But here there was no light, no sound. All was still and disorienting. She followed her instincts, letting them guide her to the bank, to where the sedges grew up. They brushed past her as she swam among them, grateful for their shelter. She swam until her lungs burned, but dared not surface. A surfacing Singer

would make a noise. And the owl was waiting. She swam until she had no choice. She must breathe. Do it quickly. Don't think. Focus.

Strife broke into the air and gulped down a silent, shuddering breath. Then she dived once more, keeping to the bank, threading her way through the sedges. Her fur, initially waterproof, now began to soak, dragging at her and weighing her down. She ignored it, swimming until she had to breathe again. A lungful, then down. Water washed coldly against her skin. She suppressed a shiver and kept going. But she was tiring fast. She had to get out.

She needed a burrow entrance. There should be many, spaced along the territory, hidden beneath the water as a refuge in times of need. Strife searched with her paws and whiskers, hunting among the hollows and roots for a hole that would lead her up and out to safety. But it was impossible. The bank was a mess of underwater roots, plant stems, and dark, peat bays. She might have passed a thousand entrances and not realized. She surfaced once more, close to the shallows. She clung to the water plants, and floated there, teeth chattering.

Above her the owl called out in the night. She shrank back among the plants.

Oh please, she thought into the darkness. *Oh, Sinethis. I can't do this. Please don't let it take me. I need help.*

She was never sure, later, whether it was really a prayer—or if it was, whether it was answered. But as she clutched the plants in the darkness, some note in the rippling water changed. The world lightened around her. Perhaps the clouds thinned, letting the moonlight through, but for a moment everything was outlined in faint silver. And across the dyke she saw a ragged-edged black hole with a flat, silvery base. A burrow. Shelter. Strife's heart leapt. Then the silver light vanished. The dyke submerged in darkness once more. But she had seen the way to safety.

A chance, then. A challenge: cross the dyke to the burrow. Strife locked its position in her mind. Only a short distance, but terribly exposed. She dared not dive. It was too dark and she was too cold. She could miss the entrance and be lost. She listened intently. No sound of the owl. This was it. *Deep breath. Come on. Move the legs. Move!* Strife released the plants and glided into the channel. She swam slowly, no splashing, with her eyes fixed on the far side. Her muscles shook. Her body was bedraggled and heavy. But the rough shape of a hole emerged from the black, filling her with hope.

Something moved in the banktop reeds. It was exactly ahead, next to the burrow. There. Again. Something waiting. If it was an enemy, exhausted as she was, it could take her. One choice. She was close enough, now. She dived for the bottom of the dyke. Three sharp strokes and she was at the dyke wall. She reached forwards, pawed at the bank, and felt . . . nothing. Her heart gave a joyful thump. A hole. Here, finally, was the lower entrance. She rushed forwards, reaching out to the sides, scrabbling at the passage walls. She pulled and kicked her way up the column of water and popped out into black air, deep in the bank's thick safety. She staggered from the water and collapsed, shivering on the floor of the tunnel. Safe. Thank Sinethis.

She climbed to her feet and moved further into the burrow. Everything smelled faintly of their mother. She was still in the territory. That was good. A nest chamber would be close by, with dry grasses and warm earth. She could sleep there. She followed the tunnel with her whiskers in the dark and, with a final effort, tottered into the chamber and curled up, wet through and shaking, in a pile of fusty grasses. The world dwindled away.

'Strife?'

She raised her head muzzily. Kale's voice. Somehow he was here. The rustling sound at the banktop. Had that been him? She tried to call out but could barely control her muscles enough to speak.

'K-Kale?'

'Strife, I'm coming.'

Kale's paws pattered through the tunnels, arrived in the chamber. His familiar presence filled the dark space.

'Are you all right? The owl. I thought it had you.'

'Am 'kay. You?'

'I'm fine. It started hunting the dyke. Too busy to see me.'

'B-busy . . . ' Strife nearly laughed, but it turned into a shudder, ' . . . h-hunting me.'

Kale moved to her side and huddled down next to her. Strife, trembling, curled around him and clung there, nestling down into his warm fur. His presence filled her with

a fierce joy. They were alive and together.

'You're cold.'

'R-r-really?' Strife managed. 'You n-noticed?' She pulled him closer. Kale said no more but simply stayed there, giving her the warmth of his body. Strife gripped him until the spasms passed. Then a warm sleepiness began to drag at her. Her eyes closed. Her head lolled . . .

. . . and Strife was brought awake by a movement at her side. It was still dark, but she had a sense that time had passed. She had slept. And there was feeling of coldness beside her. She battled the sleep that still tried to carry her away. Kale was not here. A noise close by, in the nest. Something moving.

'Kale?'

His voice at the chamber door. 'I'm still here.'

'Where are you going?'

A pause.

'Away.'

'Without me?'

'Yes.'

Anger washed through her, driving the bleariness from her mind. She shoved herself to her feet, forcing cold-stiffened muscles into action. She felt terrible: chilled and achy. But if her brother thought he could sneak off and leave her, then he was going to find out just how wrong a River Singer could be.

'Oh, were you, now?' said Strife. 'So you thought, "I know, Strife's asleep, so I can just leave and in the morning she'll be fine and I'll be off."?'

A shifting sound in the dark. 'Maybe.'

'If you haven't noticed,' she said, 'I've nearly been eaten by an owl, drowned, and frozen to death because of you.'

No answer. Strife carried on.

'So, I've just made a decision. Want to know what it is?'

'No.'

'Tough roots. I've decided that I'm going to follow you until you give me a proper reason why you want to leave. Do you like that idea, Kale?'

'Not much.'

'Thought not. So I don't suppose that you're going to tell me now and save us both the trouble?'

'No.'

Well that was just typical, wasn't it? If this evening was anything to go by Kale was probably going to keep doing stupid things until he was eaten by something with lots of teeth. Following him would probably mean the same for her but if Strife couldn't make him stay then she had no option. She shook her head in the dark. Why did he have to be so unreasonable? It didn't have to be this hard. And suddenly Strife was not just angry, she was furious: at the owl, at the blackness, and at the cold. But most of all with Kale.

'"No", he says. Great. Just brilliant.' She was fuming. 'You are a complete pain in the tail, Kale, you know that? I mean, who else would be nuts enough to find the darkest, coldest, stillest, driest night possible and go for a swim down an owl-infested dyke? Who else in the whole of the Wetted Land could possibly do something that massively stupid?'

A pause. 'Well, you did.'

Strife's mouth shut with a snap. Oh, that did it. That *really* did it. In the heat of her indignation Strife's resolve hardened to rock. He could be as stubborn and silent as he liked, but she was going with him all the way. That was all there was to it. She hunched in on herself and glowered balefully in the general direction of Kale. Moments stretched.

'Strife?' said Kale.

Strife said nothing.

'Strife?'

'Don't waste your energy. We leave at first light.'

'Strife, I—'

'And if you even consider arguing or try to leave without

me, I'll chew you into pieces and drag you back to Mother one bit at a time. Right?'

A silence.

'Right?' Strife's voice deadly quiet.

'Yes. Right,' said Kale quickly.

Strife nodded in quiet satisfaction.

'Good. Now get back here and sleep. We leave in the morning.'

Then she settled down to keep watch in the dark.

'Over here. Quickly.'

Sylvan and Fodur ran towards the sound of Aven's voice, up to the far boundary marker at the edge of her territory. Sylvan arrived first, Fodur limping up behind, making surprising speed on his three good legs. Aven and Ivy had their heads together either side of the marker.

'What is it? What have you found?'

They had been searching all morning, racing against rain that had begun again in earnest, washing the scents from the

earth. They had found no clue as to what had happened to Kale and Strife. The rain had seen to that. They were soaked and cold but there was no question of giving up. Especially not for Aven. Sylvan wouldn't want to be one of her children if they did find them. He had never seen her so afraid, angry, and determined. And now she was standing triumphantly by her boundary marker, sheltering it with her body.

'Smell this.'

Sylvan gave it a go, but the rain had scattered the feeding sign, and reduced the droppings to mush. He shook his head. 'I smell water vole. I'm sorry. I've never been good at this whole scent thing. What is it?'

'It's Strife,' said Ivy. 'She's over-marked Mother's scent, here.'

Sylvan watched Ivy's face, thoughtfully. She had been searching even harder than her mother. Almost feverishly. It was only natural that she would be upset, but she seemed to have taken everything as her own personal responsibility. She said that she had woken in the morning to find that Strife and Kale had gone. Fair enough. But Sylvan could not shake the feeling that there was something odd about her

behaviour. He wondered if she knew more about things than she was letting on.

Fodur limped forwards and scented the boundary marker. He nodded.

'Is Missy Strife. But markers is only for boss folk, yes?'

'That's right,' said Aven. 'Only territory holders get to mark. Any juveniles stupid enough to . . . ' she paused. 'Well. Let's just say that Strife tried it once. We had a little chat about it.'

'She didn't try it again, then?' said Sylvan.

'No,' said Aven grimly. 'She didn't. But now she has. Just wait until I get my paws on her.'

'Hang on,' said Sylvan. 'You don't think she did this deliberately? To get back at you, or something?'

'Not right that, methinks,' said Fodur. 'Is not like Missy Strife.'

'And before today I'd have thought that disappearing with her brother wouldn't be like her either,' said Aven bitterly. 'Looks like I was wrong about that, too. It's pure cheek. Why else would she leave a mark here?'

'I don't know,' said Sylvan, his gaze settling on Ivy. She caught him looking and shifted uncomfortably. 'How about you, Ivy,' he asked, keeping his tone light. 'Any ideas?'

Ivy stared down at the trampled grass floor. She was drenched, her fur either plastered to her body or sticking out in clumps. Here and there grass seeds lodged. She was the most dejected River Singer Sylvan had ever seen. At the question she looked even more miserable.

Aven caught the expression on her daughter's face. She stared at her.

'Ivy,' she said, 'if there's something you're not telling me, I think now would be a good time. Don't you?'

Ivy raised her head. She made a small noise.

'Maybe,' she whispered.

'Maybe,' repeated Aven, dangerously calmly. 'I'm all ears.'

Ivy swallowed. 'Strife came into the nest late last night. She said Kale had run off and asked me to help look for him. I said no, because I was angry. Then I went to sleep.'

'You went to sleep,' said Aven. Her voice was flat. 'They've been missing all night. And you went to sleep. And you only think to tell me this now?'

Ivy was shamefaced.

'How could you be so stupid?' Aven yelled. 'They've been gone all night, for Sinethis's sake. Anything could have happened to them.' She rose up and raised her paws, taking in a deep breath in preparation for more shouting.

'Aven.' Sylvan stepped swiftly in front of his sister. 'Aven, we're out in the open. Keep quiet and keep down. It's not her fault.'

Aven glowered, but sank back to the ground.

'I'm sorry, Mother,' said Ivy. 'I didn't know until I woke up, I promise.'

'You should have said something.'

'Mayhaps,' said Fodur. 'But their leaving is not Missy Ivy's fault. More is occurring here than we thinks. Why Kale be leaving? Why Strife follow? Is tricksy problem.'

'And why did Strife leave her scent here?' said Sylvan.

'She wanted you to know,' said Ivy.

They turned to her. She flinched from the attention, but said, 'If she wanted you to know she'd come this way this is what she'd do. Because there's no chance Mother would miss it.'

Aven slumped down onto her haunches.

'So they're gone,' she said

quietly. 'They're not old enough. They're not ready. My poor babies.'

Nobody spoke. They stared in silence at the slowly disintegrating boundary marker. The rain fell around them, tap-tapping from leaves and sploshing into the dyke water. The larger drops threw up strange fragments of sound, and snatches of Sinethis's song danced among them. Sylvan felt a familiar tug, deep in his gut. Sinethis pulling him away.

'I'm going after them,' said Aven.

Sylvan's eyes snapped open. 'Aven—' he began.

She rounded on him. 'Don't try to talk me out of it. I have to find them, Sylvan. They could be lost, or hurt, or anything. You don't know what it's like. You've never . . . '

She tailed off.

'I know,' said Sylvan gently. 'I don't have children. I don't know what it's like. But you still can't go.' He gestured at the boundary marker. 'If you leave you might find Strife and Kale, but what about Ivy? What about when you return? The second the other females realize you're gone you won't have anything left to get back to.'

Aven stared at Sylvan, the rain soaking her fur. Then she said, 'You're right. Of course you are.' She gazed miserably down at the earth. 'But what else can I do?'

'I'll find them,' said Sylvan. 'I was going anyway. So I'll find them and bring them back.'

He listened again to the sound of the rain on the water, and felt an echo of a familiar feeling, sending him onward. This was the right thing. He was sure of it. But then he frowned. For a moment he thought he caught a snatch of something else. Something dangerous. Almost feral. It rose up from the dyke in a spatter.

'And I comes too,' said Fodur, breaking Sylvan's concentration.

Sylvan hesitated. 'Um, no offence, Fodur, but I don't think that's a good idea. I have enough trouble moving around as a male. A male and a rat . . . not good.'

Fodur smiled. 'Knows it. But I still comes. Fodur not a know-nothing. Can help. Does things you doesn't.'

'Like?'

'I sees better at night. And I smells better.'

'That's a matter of opinion,' said Sylvan with a quick grin. 'Sorry,' he added, at Fodur's hurt look.

'Should not be making fun of rats,' said Fodur sternly. 'If Missy Strife leaving markers, mayhaps is good to have a nose? In any case Fodur a free rat. He comes.'

'I—'

'I comes,' said Fodur firmly.

Sylvan threw up his paws. 'All right. I can't see how this is going to work, but fine. If you want to come, you come.'

Fodur put a paw on Sylvan's shoulder. 'Sees? Is better when you do what the rat suggest.'

'Huh. Well I hope you know what you're doing,' said Sylvan. But even as he spoke he felt a warmth at the idea of having Fodur with him. He had been travelling alone for a long time. 'But it'll be nice to have you along.'

Fodur smiled.

'Right, Tiny,' said Sylvan to Aven, 'it looks like we have a plan. You stay here and hold the territory, we'll bring your young back.'

Aven looked from her brother to the rat with an expression of helpless gratitude. Then she straightened and groomed her wet fur. She squared her shoulders and turned to her daughter.

'Ivy, I want you back in the burrow now, please. I have a territory to maintain, and it'll be easier for me if I don't have to worry about anyone else getting lost in the rain.'

Ivy hesitated.

'If I were you,' said Aven, 'I'd be running for the burrow. You're on extremely thin leaves.'

Ivy ran. Aven turned to Sylvan and Fodur.

'As for you two: I want both of you back with my children. If anyone is going to get hurt it's going to be me doing it. I will be extremely upset if you get injured without my permission. Understood?'

Sylvan nodded. 'Yes, Aven.'

'Good. Off you go then.'

Sylvan and Fodur touched noses with her. Then they turned to leave.

'One more thing,' said Aven. 'When you find my children give them my love.'

Sylvan smiled. 'Of course.'

'Good.' Aven's eyes took on a steely glint. 'Hopefully it'll lull them into a false sense of security. Then I can deal with them properly when they're back.'

Sylvan nodded to Fodur. The pair of them stepped around Aven's marker and set off into the next territory. Just before the sedges hid Aven from view, Sylvan risked a glance back. Aven was standing where they had left her, head down, gazing into the dyke. It might have been the distance, but she seemed smaller, somehow. The sight made him even more determined. He would find Strife and Kale, and bring them home to their mother. This was his path, it seemed, and he would follow it. He turned back, following Fodur through the grasses and on into the unknown.

PART 2
SINETHIS RISING

She shelters us in her waters and burrows. She rises and dashes us. The familiar words turned over in Sylvan's mind as he stared, unseeing, out of the entrance of the disused tussock-burrow. *We are River Singers, and we are hers.* The wind had been rising steadily and now flung sheets of rain hard against the tussock wall. No let up, no mercy. Stray drops whisked in through the entrance, wetting his face. Sylvan wiped them away and scowled up at clouds. It was almost impossible to tell, but it must be near midday. Nearly time to be off. A gasping sound and a scuffle came from the chamber behind him. Sylvan spared Fodur a glance, enough to see that he had rolled onto his back, legs in the air, but was still fast asleep. Sylvan wished he could have slept too. Part of the reason he hadn't, of course, was Fodur. The rat didn't just sleep; he flipped, grunted, scratched, snorted, kicked, twitched, and flailed, all the while looking blissfully peaceful. He also snored. Loudly. Fodur had many fine points, but being a good sleeping companion was not among them.

It was not really Fodur that kept Sylvan awake, though. The wind and lashing rain had long since been loud enough to drown out his snores. No, it was everything else: the Rising, Strife, and Kale. This storm. And Sinethis. Especially Sinethis. Sylvan had grown up on the Great River where her song twined easily through her flow. But here the rain slammed into the dykes, pocking and rippling the water, and shattering Sinethis into incoherence. The torrent reduced her to a seething mess of noises, images, and feelings. No meaning. Nothing but a sense of anger that gathered with the darkening clouds. That unsettling, feral note rang out with every new flurry. It thrummed in Sylvan's head. And with every step they took it intensified.

Fodur scrabbled briefly at the burrow wall and turned onto his side. He let out a final grunt and opened his eyes. He listened for a moment, and then pulled a face.

'Ah,' he said. 'Rain is being worse, then.'

'Yes.'

'But we's going on, methinks?'

'Yes, unfortunately,' said Sylvan. 'How are you feeling?'

Fodur rolled to his feet. He stretched out his muscles and winced as the action pulled at the long-healed scar on his injured leg. He curled it up against his belly.

'Heh. Old. Damp.' He fixed Sylvan with a bright eye. 'But feisty, yes?'

Fodur's face was greying and his whiskers were sparse. He moved stiffly. If anyone had earned the right to a restful life it was him. But instead they were chasing across the Wetted Land after Aven's children.

Sylvan smiled. 'You do fine, Fodur. Travelling suits you.'

'Thinks it, does you?' Fodur limped to the entrance. He took a deep lungful of air, narrowing his eyes as rain splashed his whiskers. 'Mayhaps you has it right. Is nice to be new places. I's not ungrateful, but is tricksy among Singers.'

Sylvan knew what he meant. Travelling with a rat was not easy. He and Fodur were forced into the margins, well back from the water. They travelled at midday when the Folk were in their burrows, or at night, when Fodur's keen eyesight meant they could avoid enemies. Their only advantage was that Strife—for whatever reason—had been over-marking every female's boundary. Without this, and Fodur's nose, they would have no chance. Of course the downside was that by the time they arrived the females had discovered Strife's scent. Often they were so furious that Sylvan didn't dare go near them. Despite everything, though, he and Fodur were gaining ground. The scent was getting stronger.

A gust drove rain deep into the burrow. Fodur flattened his ears against it. He gave a wry 'Heh', then picked his way down and out of the tussock. He stood at the base, nose to the air, letting the rain soak him. Despite everything he looked like a rat that was having fun. Sylvan wondered how much Fodur had been able to get out when living with Aven, and whether the other Singers had let him be. But he shook the thoughts away and stepped from the burrow into the onslaught. He winced as the rain soaked his fur.

'Is ready?' Fodur had to raise his voice above the noise.

'No. I'm not.'

'That's what I be thinking,' Fodur grinned. 'But ready or not, here we goes.'

Fodur set off and Sylvan followed. This close to the water the rain was deafening. The wind whipped grass stems into his face. He was wet and chilled in moments. And Sinethis

battered his mind. He tried to block it out, to focus on where Fodur led, but the anger was raw. Water hissed all around him and washed at the banks. *She rises and dashes us*, he thought. It made him feel colder than the storm ever could.

'Ah!' Fodur's cry came from ahead.

'What is it?'

Fodur was standing next to the remnants of a boundary marker. It lay at the junction of two dykes: the one they were on, running straight ahead, and another, darker dyke, leading off through the trees.

'Is puplings,' Fodur called. 'Missy Strife leaves another clue.'

'And offends another female.'

'Ack, let her be. Is her way.'

'And that's a good thing?'

'She is how she is.' Fodur flicked water from his ear with a paw and smiled. 'Is the only way to be.'

Fodur put his nose to the marker once more and the smile slipped from his face. He dashed forwards a few paces down the bank, sniffing like a stoat. He shook his head and ran back. Sylvan watched, bemused, as Fodur then ran a little way down the unpleasant dyke, criss-crossing the low plants at the water's edge, checking the scents. He returned looking grave.

'Has good news and bad news.'

'What's the bad news?'

Fodur gestured up the wooded dyke with his chin. 'They goes that way.'

Sylvan's heart sank. Of course. It would have to be, wouldn't it? The dyke was a Singer's nightmare: dark trees tossing in the wind and nothing but enemies and mud below them.

'And the good news?'

'We's close. If we goes fast, fast, we catch them today.'

'Great. That way we can all be eaten together.' Sylvan scowled up at the sky. 'Not that any enemy with half a brain would be out in this.'

'You thinks?'

'No.' A gust made Sylvan stagger, slightly. He raised his voice against it. 'Come on, let's get after those pups.'

Sylvan and Fodur set off together, down the banks towards the woods. As they went the trees closed over their heads. And beyond the trees the storm gathered pace, pouring wind and rain out of a blackening sky.

'I utterly, utterly hate you,' said Strife, almost shouting to be heard. 'You do know that, don't you?'

'Yes.'

'Good. Because I do. And I mean it and everything.'

They huddled in a scant stand of sedges, pressed together against freezing rivulets and spraying rain. Kale stared ahead down the dyke, lost in thought. Despite Strife's best and most persistent questioning he had refused to tell her where they were going. Or *why* they were going. Or anything, for that matter.

'I mean,' she yelled, 'there's no shelter, I'm cold, I'm drenched and I can barely hear myself speak—'

'Lucky you,' Kale muttered.

'—there are no Singers and we're in the middle of nowhere. Why can't we find a proper burrow? Why can't we go home?'

Home seemed a long way away now. Especially down this dyke. Trees crowded close to the water, as if jostling to dip their roots into it. Branches waved and crashed overhead. Rain rattled through them or blew down from the leaves in big drops. It splashed into the dyke, causing the green surface scum to swirl and ripple; it smacked heavily onto the ground; it hit Strife, stinging viciously. There was no escape. Here and there small stands of reeds were being thrashed to rags by the wind, or clusters of low broad-leaved plants bobbed and jiggled. Everything else was bare earth. An unhappy feeling clenched in Strife's gut. They should not be here. She should turn, and run back to the marsh. These were woods. For enemies: not for Singers.

'Finished moaning?' asked Kale. Strife's lips tightened. He ignored her expression and nodded away down the dyke to a small, flattened stand of reeds at the water's edge.

'There,' he shouted. 'The next shelter.'

And before Strife could speak he ran from the sedges. She had no option but to follow. They dashed together through the dancing broad-leaves, skirting the dark places where the plants were thin. When they paused, Strife's muscles tensed, ready to flee or to fight. They ran to the stand of reeds and ducked into it. As they entered, Strife's paw came down on something brittle that snapped beneath her weight. She leapt away, stifling a squeak. Where she had stepped a small pile of bones and sodden fur clung to the soil.

'What's that?' asked Kale.

Strife batted at the grisly mess with her paw. A small, white bone rolled out of it.

'Oh, this.' She tried to keep calm. 'Nothing, really. Just some bones. You know, like what we're going to be if we keep going down here.'

Kale looked at it for some moments and then gave a small shrug. Strife stared at him.

'You don't get it, do you?' she shouted. 'Look around

you, Kale. Look at the trees, these bones. This place is death for Singers. If we don't freeze in the rain we're going to be gobbled up by the enemies. Is that what you want?'

'I'll be fine.'

Strife's breath hissed between her teeth. 'What did you say?' Her voice rose to a shriek. '*You'll* be fine?'

Kale nodded. 'Yes.'

'Oh, I'm *so* glad to hear it.' She took a step towards him. 'And what about me?' she demanded. 'I mean, it's nice to know that you'll be OK. It'll be a consolation when I'm being chewed up by a fox. I'll think *it's a shame the fox is eating me but at least Kale's fine.*'

'I didn't ask you to be here,' Kale snapped.

Strife tensed, ready to yell at him or batter him with her paws, anything to get through his thick head. But then she stopped dead. Kale too stiffened, gazing up at the trees. Both of them went still: listening, watching. Something in the note of the storm had changed. The rain eased, and the wind swirled uncertainly as, for a moment, the savage beating abated. The air grew heavy, expectant almost. Kale and Strife exchanged glances. Whatever this was, it did not feel good.

A deep rumble, right at the edge of hearing. Strife craned for a view of the sky. Through gaps in the waving branches she saw clouds that were black and twisted round on themselves. They were shot through with veins of white and deep almost-purple, and they circled, pressing closer together. Any bright spaces between them were squeezed from existence. The light began to fail.

'I don't like this,' said Strife.

Kale said nothing. But he swallowed nervously.

From far away back down towards the marsh came a roaring noise. A gust hurtled the length of the dyke, smashing through the treetops as it came. One after another the trees began to shake. Chill air slammed into Strife with a blast that flattened the broad-leaves and reeds. Strife was knocked to all fours. She crouched low and clung to the soil as branches clattered overhead. And then it passed, leaving her gasping. She staggered to Kale and gripped him tightly.

'Kale,' she shouted. 'I—'

The sky flashed blinding white. The trees threw stark,

black shadows that flickered on the ground. Strife squeaked. And a terrible sound boomed out across the woods; a deep growl that seemed to come from everywhere. It echoed and rolled among the trees. It clamoured around them before passing over and away. It faded to silence leaving the River Singers wide-eyed.

Strife raked the landscape for the danger, seeking an escape. What could make a sound like that? It had been huge, savage, powerful. Strife felt her rapid breathing, the pulse in her throat. She wanted to run but was terrified to stillness. Light flashed across the clouds once more. And moments later another boom. The wind howled, driving fresh rain before it. Sounds were obliterated by a patter, then a hammering that battered at plants, soil, and Singers alike, stinging on noses, paws, eyes. Strife huddled against Kale, vainly trying to shield herself. Then Kale's paws were beneath her forelegs, tugging her upright.

'Come on,' he shouted. 'We have to move.'

'Move?' Strife yelled. 'Where to?'

'Come on!'

The sky flashed. Strife half staggered and was half dragged to her feet. Even here in the reeds it was difficult to stand. Thunder bellowed above her. Wind ripped at her fur, pummelled the plants, and flung dyke-water in her face. The trees flailed in

She clambered through them, grabbing for twigs, using the tree to scramble back up the bank. She emerged into devastation. The dyke was filled with a tangle of broken and twisted branches, flattened broad-leaves, and crushed sedges. Strife stood amid what must have been the very topmost twigs of the highest branch. The damage ended almost exactly at her feet. She swallowed. If she had run any slower the tree would have crushed her.

'Strife!' Kale's voice, half lost in the rain. 'Strife!'

Strife could do nothing but stare. She could have been killed. She was dimly aware of Kale behind her. She could hear, too, that the storm had quietened, that it was moving away. She knew, vaguely, that she should be watching for danger. But still she could do nothing but stare.

Kale scampered up. 'Strife . . . you're OK! Thank Sinethis.'

She did not respond. He pattered around her. Kale's worried face filled her view.

'Strife?'

He put a paw on her shoulder. She let it rest there, rocking back with his weight.

'Are you all right?'

'A tree,' she said weakly. 'A tree.'

'Yes,' said Kale, carefully. 'It's a tree, Strife. That's right.'

Strife blinked. Something in his tone sparked inside her. Anger. She was feeling angry. She took a deep breath. Then, with great deliberation, she lifted a paw and smacked Kale hard across the head. He yelped. She grabbed him and put her nose right against his.

'A tree fell on me,' Strife shouted. 'Because of you, Kale. A *tree*. I could have been killed. If we ever get out of this I will never speak to you again.'

Then Strife let him go and set about grooming her fur into some semblance of order. It didn't work very well, but the action made her feel better.

'Now,' she said finally, 'can you give me one good reason why we shouldn't just turn around and head back?'

'Yes,' said Kale. 'There. Look.'

Kale pointed with his chin past her. Strife turned to follow the gesture. More broad-leaves and trees. More dark dyke edge. Brilliant. The best reason to go home she had ever seen. But then she saw what he was pointing at. The woods ahead had a thin quality. Their shade was less deep, somehow, and behind them lay a hint of open sky. They must have reached the edge of the trees. And despite everything something like hope began to grow in her. Whatever was ahead, it had to be better than where they were. Or did it? She shot Kale a suspicious glance.

'So, that's the end of the woods, is it? And I trust that there's an enormous burrow filled with warm grass and tasty roots waiting for us the other side?'

Kale put his head on the side and gazed at her. 'Beyond here is the Great River. I think there'll be a burrow.'

Strife goggled. '*What*?'

'Come on.'

Kale set off, leaving Strife gaping in his wake. How could he possibly know that? She scuttled after him.

'What did you mean about the Great River?' she demanded.

'You'll see. Just wait.'

Strife sprinted ahead of her brother and whipped around to face him. She put her forepaws on his shoulders and shoved him back in his tracks. She was so infuriated that she actually started jumping up and down in front of him.

'I-don't-want-to-wait-just-tell-me-what's-happening-you-complete-bonehead.'

'I can't. Just trust me. We'll get out of these woods and it'll be fine. Trust me. Please?'

Kale was almost begging. Strife regarded him for long

moments. Then she released his shoulders and sank slowly back to all fours.

'All right,' she said, finally. 'You have one more chance. But if any more trees fall on me that's it. Right?'

An expression almost of relief passed across Kale's face. For a moment Strife thought he might even thank her. But then he simply nodded, once, and set off. He scurried briskly down through the broad-leaves towards the edge of the woods. Strife took a breath and followed him. This, she thought, had better be good.

'Well, I have to hand it to you, Kale. For a moment there I was all ready to head home.' Strife settled down to glare at the landscape. 'I'm *so* glad I decided to trust you instead.'

They were in a measly clump of grasses right at the edge of the trees. To either side the woodland edge stretched away in a neat line, as if all of the trees had got together and simply decided to stop. And if they had, Strife thought, she wouldn't blame them. A few steps in front of her lay the most horrible landscape she had ever seen. No river. No burrow. Instead the dyke continued on through a vast, flat expanse of short-cropped grasses. The end of the field, if it even had an end, was hidden by grey flurries of rain. No food or shelter, not even on the dyke banks. Apart from one distant, short stand of sedges the dyke was a devastated, muddy pulp, pitted with craters big enough for a Singer to swim in. Kale had brought her to a broad, frothing quagmire in a barren field.

'You really are a bonehead.'

Kale did not even look at her. He kept on gazing in dismay at the field. The sky flashed and rumbled in the distance. The main storm had moved off, dragging behind it a wet tail of rain. But Strife knew that neither of them would cross such a space.

'I was so sure.' Kale's voice was quiet, almost a whisper. 'She led me here.'

'*She* led you here?' said Strife, flatly. 'And who's "she", exactly?'

No response.

'Look,' said Strife, 'don't you think it's about time you told me what's happening?'

Kale's head came up, slowly. He gazed at Strife, as if assessing her. 'Maybe,' he said. Then he closed his eyes briefly. 'All right.' He took a breath. 'Ever since the rain started I knew I had to leave. I had a feeling,'—he tapped his ribs —'here.'

Strife stared at him.

'And there were words and things,' Kale continued, 'but sort of garbled. Like they should make sense, except the rain had . . . blurred them or something. I understood enough to know that she wanted me to come to the river. That everything would be all right if I did.' He shrugged and made a small sound, almost a laugh. 'So that's it. You think it sounds stupid, don't you?'

Strife nodded, not trusting herself to speak.

'Knew you would,' he said. 'I tried so hard to ignore it, Strife. But then I heard Sylvan talking about Sinethis and for the first time it was like it wasn't only me, like the words were real and everything would be all right.' He sighed and gazed out at the rain. 'And now look.'

So that was it: strange feelings and broken words in Kale's head. And for that Strife had left home, been hunted by an owl, and nearly been crushed under a tree. Part of her wanted to shout at him, or demand an apology and tell him he was an idiot again. But what would that achieve? Now she knew his reasons, as stupid as they were, she found it hard to be properly angry. Kale watched her face for a moment. Then he lowered his head onto his paws.

'I'm sorry,' he said. He looked so dejected that Strife almost began to feel sorry for him. Almost.

'Right. Well,' she said, as kindly as she could manage. 'This place is too dangerous to hang around. So what are we going to do?'

'I don't know,' Kale mumbled. 'I don't know what to do.'

Strife straightened. 'Then I think it's time we headed

home. Unless you really fancy crossing that?'

Kale's eyes flicked to the horizon. 'Maybe—' he began. But then he stopped, and looked away. 'No,' he said. 'I don't. I'm sorry.'

Strife gave him a sharp look. For a moment she was unsure who the apology was meant for. But then she put a paw on Kale's shoulder and smiled.

'OK,' she said. 'Let's wait for the wind to drop a bit further. Then if we're lucky we can still get back to the main dyke by darkness. Now, let's see if we can get ourselves a bit . . . '

She tailed off. At the far limit of sight some movement caught her eye. It was nearly impossible to see, but a patch of greyness resolved itself, just for a moment, into lighter and darker shapes. They looked huge, but distant. Strife rubbed at her eyes and peered out into the shifting rain. But the shapes had vanished. Only the field and dyke remained, empty but for that useless stand of sedges.

'What is it?' asked Kale.

Strife shook her head, slowly, still staring away. 'Nothing,' she said. 'I must have imagined it.' Even so Strife didn't feel like sitting there any more. 'OK, I'm cold and wet and if we stay here I'm going to start seeing things. Or hearing voices,' she added, giving Kale a meaningful look. 'So I say we get going.'

She stood with difficulty, forcing her bruised and cold-stiffened muscles to work. She staggered around, turning her back to the ghastly field. After a moment Kale joined her.

'Back to the woods,' she said. 'Goody.'

An odd movement in the broad-leaves caught her eye. It was difficult to see in the breeze, but just for a moment the plants looked as though they were being pushed apart. She frowned, focusing on the place. There. A ripple in among the stems, moving against the wind. Something was heading towards them up the dyke. Something was coming.

'Can you see that?' Strife hissed.

Kale next to her was alert, tense. He nodded once.

'What do you think it is?' said Strife. 'Fox?'

'Too small. Stoat. Or polecat.'

An enemy. Please, no. Not here. The ripple moved again, closer now. Something sniffing its way up through the broad-leaves. It was following their scent, and if they stayed here it would find them. But where could they go? Not into the woods. The dyke was their only protection. If they left it . . . she shuddered.

'Strife. There. That way.'

Kale's gaze was fixed on the lone, distant stand of sedges on the dyke edge.

'No,' said Strife. 'No way. Not into the field. There's no cover. We'll be taken.'

'We will if we stay here.'

Strife glanced back to the woods. The movement in the broad-leaves was clearer. Closer. She wrenched her gaze back to the far sedges. Too open, she thought. But a chance. No choice. Right.

Strife stepped from the grasses and out onto the mud of the dyke edge. The fur along her spine bristled. She had never been in the open before. She felt the chill of exposure, the ghost of an enemy's claws at her back. She sensed, rather than saw, Kale fall in behind her. She hunched low, trying not to be seen, keeping her eyes locked on the sedges. Their only chance was to get to those plants. She twisted between the ruts and pits as, step by cautious step, her paws dragged her towards the cover. It was interminable. Only when she parted the first leaves, and the reassuring closeness of the tall sedge-blades pressed around them, did Strife allow herself to breathe. Kale crept in behind. For long moments they merely stayed there, pressed together, letting the fear ebb away. Then Strife turned to face the woods.

'Kale, whatever comes out of those woods, I want you to know something.'

'What?'

'This is *your* fault.'

Kale said nothing, but stared tensely back across the field. *Please*, Strife thought. *Please, whatever-you-are, just leave us alone.* For a moment she half hoped that her prayer had been answered. But then she spied a stir in the grasses. The clump moved as though some animal were sniffing in it. A greyish muzzle poked cautiously out. It lifted, scenting. It hesitated, and withdrew. And then the plants parted and two figures slunk into view. One was slight and brownish. The other was larger and greyer, nose to the ground. They moved together, skirting the muddied edge of the dyke, creeping toward the sedges where Strife and Kale waited. They disappeared for a moment behind a rut. But not before Strife got her first clear look at them.

'Hah!' Strife sagged back onto her haunches, flooding with relief. All this time she had been hoping that someone had followed her markers. And now, almost beyond hope, she had seen Sylvan and Fodur picking their way down the dyke edge. She burst out laughing. Kale gave her an odd look.

'What's funny?'

'It's just . . . ' Strife pulled herself together. 'Well, I don't think they're going to eat us. Do you?'

'Dunno,' said Kale. He watched them thoughtfully. 'Looks like Sylvan might.'

She saw what he meant. Strife could just about make out her uncles' expressions, and they didn't look happy. Well, that was fair enough. She wasn't exactly ecstatic herself.

'Maybe if he eats you first he won't have room for me.'

But Kale was not listening. Instead he was staring away to another part of the field.

'Strife!' his voice was full of urgency. 'Strife. Look.'

'Oh, *now* what?' Kale's paw was on her shoulder, turning her.

'Look!'

98

The wind blew rain across the field in grey tatters. It lifted the haze and left clear patches in its wake. And through them Strife could now see the shapes of beasts, black and white and gigantic. She felt muscles clench in her back. These creatures were immense, crowding the far edge of the field in a colossal herd. Some of them split away, moving down the border of the woods in a ragged line. The others followed. The beasts tossed their great heads as they went, and their flanks steamed in the air. Hooves sank into wet earth, leaving the ground ripped and scarred where they passed. And now Strife, eyes fixed on those ragged pits, knew what had destroyed the dyke banks. Abruptly, one of the beasts started at the wind. It kicked up its hind legs and staggered in a clumsy circle. Its neighbours shied, skittishly. Then they settled back into line, and the herd trod its path together, moving down towards the dyke.

Strife glanced quickly over at Sylvan and Fodur, still in the open, making for the sedges. She looked back at the creatures. The leader reached the dyke edge. It lowered its head to the mud and swept from side to side. Then it stretched out its neck and bellowed into the air. Strife saw its white-pink tongue, and the steam of its breath. Heads raised among the following creatures, and a number of bellows answered. Strife took an involuntary step backwards, deeper under cover. The lead creature turned to stare down the length of the dyke. It spotted Sylvan and Fodur's tiny forms. It called again and began to lumber forwards. The herd followed, first at a walk, then a straggling canter. The jumbled sound of their tread rose above the wind. And the sodden soil beneath Strife's paws began to tremble.

Strife watched, powerless, as Sylvan and Fodur stopped and whirled to face the creatures. They stared for an instant and then turned and fled, dashing in crazy zigzags to where she and Kale cowered. Behind them, in a confusion of hooves, galloped the beasts. The creatures moved with ghastly speed. Sylvan and Fodur sprinted ahead with grim determination. Strife's own muscles clenched, urging them onward.

Sylvan and Fodur burst through the sedges and staggered to a stop, chests heaving and ears flat. They took in Strife and Kale's presence in an instant. Then they then whipped about to face their pursuers. The herd pounded closer, never slowing. Strife gaped in terror. The cover of these sedges meant nothing; they would be obliterated in an instant. Sylvan shouted something, pointing at the back of the stand. Kale leapt to obey. Fodur backed into Strife, who began to turn, ready to flee. The ground shook. Their view filled with legs and churning mud. Kale was clawing at something; Sylvan was at the far edge, yelling frantically.

A gust of wind rattled through the sedges, forcing them aside. For a horrible instant the screen of stems was whipped away and Strife stood exposed before the plunging hooves. Then the gust passed, and the sedges snapped upright. The lead creature's head jerked up, spooked by the movement. It planted its hooves, straight-legged into the ground and skidded to a halt, tearing up the turf. Confusion spread through the beasts' ranks. And in a muddle of barging, jostling and shoving, the charge was done. The herd stood, as if unsure of what to do, right at the edge of the sedges.

Sylvan gave a mirthless laugh. Strife sagged to the ground.

'Ah,' Fodur gasped. 'Is good, that. I be thinking we's in trouble.' Then he turned to Strife and Kale and put his head on the side. 'And looks. We finds puplings.'

'Apparently so,' said Sylvan tersely. He was at the back of the sedges, checking ahead down the dyke. Strife watched the beasts as they bunched together, all snorting nostrils and whisking tails. Occasionally one nudged forward, only to shove back again, eyes rolling. Each time a hoof hit the ground Strife felt the vibration through her paws.

Strife moved closer to Fodur. 'Just what are those things meant to be?' she hissed. 'Are they enemies?'

Fodur shook his head. 'No. Is cows,' he said.

'Is grass-eaters, like Singers.'

'So why were they chasing you?'

'Cows chases anything. They's bored.'

'Oh, that's good,' said Strife brightly. 'So maybe they're not too dangerous.'

Fodur gave her a look. 'Unless they tramples you. Then things be getting squishy.'

One of the cows broke out of the huddle and pranced up to the sedges. It crushed some of the plants beneath its hooves. It gave an experimental sniff then recoiled, throwing up a spray of earth.

'Unless they trample us, eh?' said Sylvan from behind them. 'Then I think we've been here long enough. It's time to go.'

'Definitely,' said Strife. 'But where?'

'Down the dyke. It's the only way.'

No. She wanted to go home. 'But—' she began.

'But nothing,' Sylvan snapped. 'These cows are between us and the woods. If we don't want to be stamped flat we have to get to the river.'

Kale raised his head. 'River?' He turned a hope-filled face to Sylvan. 'The Great River?'

'Yes,' said Sylvan. 'The Great River. She runs past this field.'

One of the cows called out, a long, deep note that sent a shiver down Strife's spine.

'Come on,' said Sylvan. He sniffed the air once then stepped out of the back of the sedges. Strife hesitated. The cow called again, this time with a rising note. It was answered by more calls from within the herd.

'Time to be moving, yes?' said Fodur in Strife's ear. 'Fast, fast.'

Strife heard hooves. *Stamped flat*, she thought. *Squishy*. And in an instant she was out and scampering along the muddy dyke. From behind came a tearing and sniffing as sedges were ripped apart by inquisitive cows. Strife put her head down and kept moving. The Great River was close. Sylvan had said so. And Kale had been right after all. *Stop thinking. Run*. In front of her Fodur, Kale, and Sylvan were pulling away. Strife urged her aching muscles faster.

A line of ragged shapes rose up ahead of them from the grey. They resolved into battered-looking banks and cropped green plants. And beyond those, more plants and a long glitter of water. Strife's heart leapt. The Great River. Safety. But even as she thought it, she realized that the ripping noises had stopped, replaced by the drum of hooves. Oh, Sinethis. The cows were coming. She urged her legs to go faster. Ahead of her Sylvan reached the shore. He turned, shouting encouragement. Kale and Fodur staggered up behind him, joining the shout. But their voices were drowned out by the approaching herd. The Great River surged closer, a band of silver just beyond reach. She was going to make it.

A rut snagged her hind foot. She tripped, rolled,

scrambled to her feet. She was up and running in an instant. But in the delay the herd was past her and wheeling back. She spun to face the dyke, ready to dive. But cows splashed into it, spraying up water and mud. And in moments she was surrounded, cut off from both river and dyke by a forest of legs and lowered heads. The cows formed a circle, sniffing curiously. Moist nostrils, sweet breath, and steam. Strife spun this way and that, seeking any gap. But there was none. She stood up on her hind legs, squeaking defiance.

'Go away,' she shouted. 'Leave me alone!'

The herd pressed in. Strife whacked her paws at any nose that came close enough. Some flinched away, but one sidled closer. Its breath ruffled her fur. Its mouth opened, showing rows of blunt teeth and a green-stained tongue. Then the head came round and for long moments an eyeball the size of Strife's face swivelled at her. And then it was the nose again, sniffing. The cow blew out a gust of warm air that flecked her whiskers. Strife flinched, and tensed. She bared her teeth. Closer. Sniffing. Closer.

And Strife leapt, grabbing and biting at anything she could reach.

The cow roared with pain and yanked away. It stumbled and barged into those behind. They staggered back and a gap opened in their ranks. Through it Strife saw earth and plants. And beyond, the Great River. She bolted for it, screaming in fear and anger. They reared back, startled by the tiny yelling Singer. A flurry of steps, and with a final immense effort Strife launched. Grasses, water, and mud wheeled dizzyingly. Her body tumbled. She crashed through reeds, struck the bank, bounced. And splashed face first into glorious water.

She kicked out, twisting instinctively, trying to turn the roll into a dive. In the Wetted Land it would have worked. But these were no tame dyke waters. Here the water roiled. It pulled her one way and then batted her another. She gasped, shoving back at these strange forces, fending them off. But they were relentless. She bobbed to the surface. She glimpsed the far bank. It was impossibly distant. Strife swam, thrusting against the currents and cutting across the flow. The noise was unlike anything she had heard: massive and unbelievably powerful, with deep notes, trills, and snatches of melody. The sounds entered her mind, at once alien and familiar. They towered around her, thundering and filling her with their danger and rage. But even so they spoke to something she had never known existed; a deep sense of belonging, as if for all of the anger, this was her place. The conflicting senses mounted until the torrent seemed to run both through and around her. Sinethis battered her mind and body, threatening to carry her away from herself.

'Stop,' cried Strife. 'Please, stop.'

And instantly the feeling was gone. Sinethis was a river once more. The water flowed strongly, but the bank could be reached. She swam and, stroke-by-stroke, the land came closer. The current buffeted her but she fought it with grim determination. It released her, and soon she bobbed out into calm waters beneath a thick roof of sweet-grass. She grasped two pawfuls of plants and heaved herself up onto the bank, shaky but alive. Hah! Cow! Try to eat her, would it? She hoped its nose fell off. Hah, tree, you won't get me! She had lived through a storm, dodged a tree, bitten a cow, and battled the Great River. She had run, fought, and survived. Hah.

But somewhere inside, behind her racing heart and hysterical triumph, she knew that she had been lucky. Any of those things could have snapped out her life in an instant. And although she would never admit it, that frightened her to her core. As her breathing calmed, Strife slumped back against the thick grasses. Her gaze travelled back across the river. What she saw took her breath away. The far bank was a ragged line of mud and grasses. And in front of it water moved hypnotically downflow. The Great River captured the murky daylight and cast it back in uncountable glimmering facets. Strife made a small noise. Nobody had ever told her that Sinethis would be beautiful. Lost in her reverie, she barely noticed the movement behind her, or the paws that reached down and gently helped her up the bank and into deep cover.

Reluctantly she turned away, and allowed herself to be escorted into the sweet-grass. She clambered up to be greeted by the sight of two bedraggled, panting River Singers and a half-drowned rat. They too had escaped. Strife blinked stupidly at their faces: Kale sheepish, Fodur worried, Sylvan angry. She wanted to laugh. She wanted to curl up. Words came, unasked, from her mouth.

'Where are we?'

'The Great River,' replied Sylvan. 'And if you feel like surviving the night we should find some shelter.'

For some reason one of Strife's paws started to tremble. She put it on the ground, quickly. Sylvan peered at her closely. His expression softened.

'Are you all right?' he asked. 'The cows didn't hurt you or anything?'

Strife straightened her back and stared him straight in the eye.

'No,' she said. 'I mean yes. Of course. I'm fine.'

She was proud of how she kept her voice steady—but then her body ruined everything by bursting into tears.

Sylvan was unhappy. Strife knew this because he had been going on about *exactly* how unhappy he was all evening. Even Strife, who considered herself an expert at being told-off, thought his performance was impressive. But it wasn't very fair. Of course he and Uncle Fodur had nearly been trampled, but it wasn't like she had wanted to come here. And they had only found her and Kale because of the marks she'd been leaving. If anyone should be apologizing for anything it was Kale—and he clearly wasn't going to. She sneaked a look at her brother. His face was completely impassive. The sight made Strife's paws itch. Ever since they had found the Great River his expression had been almost smug. Any self-doubt had vanished.

'So,' Sylvan concluded. 'Do you have anything to say for yourselves?'

Strife caught Kale's eye. He shrugged. Nothing to add, apparently. Right.

'Yes,' said Strife. 'Actually I do. This wasn't my idea and you shouldn't be shouting at me. I kept telling Kale to go home but he wouldn't.' She fixed Kale with her most disapproving look. 'Because he's a bonehead.' She turned back to Sylvan. 'Also your whiskers waggle when you're angry.'

From the corner of her eye she saw Uncle Fodur's expression, half amused, half disapproving. Sylvan's brows drew down into a scowl. For a moment she thought he might yell at her. But then he sighed. He groomed his whiskers for a moment then said, 'I wasn't aware of that. Thank you for pointing it out.'

She couldn't quite believe she'd got away with that.

'You're welcome,' she said. 'I've noticed lots of other things about you too, if you'd like to know?'

'I'm sure they're fascinating. Tell me: while you were busy noticing things, did you spot anything unusual about this burrow?'

'Like what?'

'Like the fact that it's deserted?'

She had been trying not to think about that. Kale had found the burrow entrance a little way from where they surfaced. It had been so buried among the overgrown grasses that they'd had to force their way in. Then Sylvan and Uncle Fodur had put her in one of the nest chambers to recover after that embarrassing crying thing. When the shaking had passed she had gone for an explore. She returned feeling odd. Everything about the burrow said that it had once belonged to Singers. The banks were higher, and the tunnels deeper and drier, but otherwise it could have been the burrow she grew up in. Singers would have been happy here, once. But now the tunnels had fallen, blocked with piles of earth. Roots twisted through the walls, and the entrances were barred by brambles. The lower levels were filled with river water. And there were no Singers' scents. She suppressed a shudder. The burrow was empty. It was wrong.

'Oh, I noticed that,' she said. 'I'm not stupid you know.'

'I haven't seen much evidence of that.' He raised a forestalling paw. 'Look, have you thought about *why* it might be deserted?'

Strife opened her mouth. Then she shut it, and shook her head. It was Kale who supplied the answer.

'Mink,' he said.

'Exactly,' said Sylvan. 'Mink.'

Mink. The beast from the stories. The word sounded strange, here in the reality of this burrow.

'That?' said Strife. 'I thought you killed it.'

'No,' said Sylvan. 'I didn't kill the mink any more than you killed a cow. An otter killed it. But who ever said there's only one of them? Why do you think we left the Great River in the first place?'

Something about the expression on his face scared her more than any amount of shouting. The mink was real. It had lived here. It had taken these Singers' lives. Strife felt

as though something were
creeping up her spine. She
resisted the urge to glance around
the chamber to see if there was a
mink behind her.

'Are there more?'

'Maybe. I don't know. But I don't think
we should stay here and find out. First thing
in the morning we're getting off the river and
I'm taking you home.'

'That's fine by me,' said Strife, eyeing Kale.
'I never wanted to come here anyway.'

Back to the marsh. Strife could barely
wait. Nothing about this place was right, and
that included the river. Strife had seen Sinethis,
now, and heard her. And Strife didn't trust her.
As beautiful as Sinethis was, Strife remembered
too clearly the anger and the power. Sinethis rushed
downflow in brown haste, heedless and selfish. She
poured past the burrow's middle entrances, and
swirled around the lower levels. She chewed at the
banks, carrying away clods of soil. She wasn't safe.
A river like that could do anything she
wanted.

Sylvan turned to Fodur. 'What

do you say, Fodur? Home?'

'Is right, that,' said Fodur. But Strife noticed a slight pause before he said it. Odd, she thought. It almost sounded as if he didn't want to go back. But before she could think further about it, Kale spoke.

'No,' he said.

Sylvan blinked. 'No? What do you mean "no"?'

'No,' said Kale. 'I'm not going.'

Strife rounded on her brother. 'That does it. I knew you were nuts after the woods, but this is ridiculous. Didn't you hear him? There might be more mink here. You can't run away from a mink. It'll take you. And I'm beginning to think you deserve it.'

'I know,' said Kale with infuriating calmness. 'But I have to be here.'

Strife was incensed.

'Stop saying things like that!' she shouted. 'I'm fed up to my back teeth of you being all—'

'Strife,' said Sylvan, interrupting. 'Just give me a second, will you.' He was looking at Kale in a narrow, appraising way. 'What do you mean you *have* to be here?'

Kale cocked his head almost as if listening to something. He gave a slight nod then said, 'I have to be here. And so do you, I think.'

'Any particular reason?'

But Kale simply shook his head. 'You know the reason,' he said. 'I'm going to find a nest for the night. Everything will be clear in the morning.'

Kale made a small, almost apologetic movement of the head and left the chamber. Sylvan watched him go in bewilderment.

'Is he always like this?' Sylvan demanded.

'Oh, he's always been a pest,' said Strife. 'But he's been worse since the stuff you said about the Rising.'

Strife's mouth shut with a snap. A paw came instinctively up to her face before she whisked it from view. She beamed at Sylvan and Fodur hoping they hadn't noticed anything.

'"Stuff I said about the Rising", eh?' said Sylvan, catching Fodur's eye. Fodur frowned at Strife.

'Knows things, does you?'

'Oh, not really,' said Strife with a winning smile. 'Only from your wonderful stories, Uncle Fodur.'

Fodur did not smile. 'Is not good to sweet-talk the rat. I trickses ratlings before you was born. You listens to private talks, methinks?'

Oh dear.

'Only a little bit. We were curious.'

'Curious, heh? And what is it that you hears?'

Strife backed away, still trying to look innocent. 'Oh, nothing much. Just something about Sinethis calling and something about something rising and a bit about Aunt Fern. That's all.'

Both of her uncles were frowning. Strife braced for a shouting-at. But instead Sylvan gazed away down the tunnel that Kale had just taken.

'Kale heard about Sinethis and the Rising. And he left the burrow.'

'Yes,' said Strife.

'Good,' said Sylvan absently, still staring away. 'We'll, I think you had better go after him. Get some sleep and we'll talk tomorrow.'

'But—'

'Now you should not be talking,' said Fodur sternly. 'You's not wanting to make Fodur unhappy. He's not an approving rat.'

'Right, right,' said Strife hurriedly. 'I'll find Kale and go to sleep. I'm actually really tired anyway. Long day, lots of cows, that sort of thing.' She took another step backwards. 'Well, goodnight, then.'

She turned and scampered a little way down the tunnel. But, out of habit she stopped just out of sight around the corner. She kept her feet going, just for good measure, to make it sound like she was still moving away. She held her breath, listening to their conversation.

'Puplings. Heh. What you thinks?'

'I don't know,' said Sylvan. 'But there's something happening, here. Kale knows something.'

'But about what? Sinethis, you thinks?'

'Maybe. But I have a nasty feeling that we're going to find out.' Sylvan let out a breath. 'Look, there's nothing we can do right now and I'm tired. Let's get some sleep. Are you all right to sleep here?'

'Ack. Night sleeping. Not good for rats.'

'I know. Sorry.'

'Mayhaps I finds other place. Spares you the snores.'

Sylvan laughed. 'OK. Thanks.'

Strife heard Fodur leave the chamber and Sylvan start to collect bedding. Time to be going. She padded off to find Kale, following his scent up to a small chamber right at the top of the burrow. He was already asleep in a pile of old grass, and she nestled next to him like a pup. Below them and beyond the wall Sinethis raced, carving her way downflow. In the burrow-quiet the sounds multiplied and echoed until the world was all darkness and Sinethis. Strife felt almost afraid to sleep. Something about the river was unfriendly, and foreboding. Eventually exhaustion welled up claiming her more surely than the deepest water. And when she dreamed it was of anger, and of drowning.

Sylvan awoke, head pounding. Sinethis roared in his mind. He clutched at his skull, staggering upright. He cradled his head, trying to rid himself of the pain and the noise. Sinethis was not singing, she was howling like a beast. She lashed and tore at him until there was nothing in Sylvan but fury. And then she passed, leaving him gasping. Sylvan panted, huddled against the earth as the Great River fell away. Something was terribly wrong. He rolled upright and listened. Through the burrow wall Sinethis's waters raged. The sound was all around him. But he was in a high chamber. The river could not possibly be this high. Not unless . . .

Water sheeted thinly across the floor. It swirled around Sylvan's legs and slipped away. It was instantly followed by another wash, higher this time. This too ebbed, leaving Sylvan spluttering with shock and cold. He scrabbled at the wet earth, dragging himself to his feet. Water in the burrow!

Sinethis was flooding. *Fodur. The children.* He had to get to them. The blackness, though, was disorienting. Everywhere was the smell of earth and river, and the ebb and rush of water overlying the background roar. He staggered blindly across the chamber, stumbling as a fresh influx took his legs from under him. He fell badly against the wall, smacking his head against it. New pain, but no time for that. The wall would keep him on his feet. He could follow it.

Sylvan stumbled to the tunnel that led to Fodur's chamber. The floor sloped upwards but even as his feet made contact with it a wash dragged at his paws. Sylvan clawed for purchase, fighting the water's grip, and hauled himself up to the higher ground. A terrible gurgling sound rose out of the burrow below as Sinethis poured through its narrow spaces. Sylvan sprinted for Fodur's nest. He burst in, yelling Fodur's name, struggling to make himself heard over the growing tumult. Water followed him, spreading across the floor. He skidded and splashed, colliding with the unseen rat in the dark.

'Whatzit?' Fodur shouted.

'Fodur! It's me. Are you OK?'

'I's wet, what happens?'

'The river's flooding. We've got to get out of here.'

Even as he spoke more water poured through the chamber.

'Which way?' said Fodur.

'The lower levels have gone. We've got to get higher.'

'Puplings? Is they here?'

'No,' said Sylvan. 'They went into the main burrow. I don't know where they are.'

'We searches?'

'We don't have time. We've got to get out.'

Fodur was aghast. 'But the puplings.'

'They're Singers. They'll find their way.'

'No,' said Fodur. 'I finds them. I helps.'

Sylvan grabbed two pawfuls of the rat's hair.

'Listen to me,' he shouted, 'if we don't leave now we won't be helping anyone. Do you understand? It'll kill us.'

A wave slammed through the chamber, scouring the soil from beneath them. They tottered against the wall and Fodur slid from Sylvan's grasp. He fell bodily into the water as it receded. Sylvan clutched blindly for his friend, heaving him up before the water could pull him out of the chamber. Fodur's paws scrabbled at the mud as Sylvan brought him back to his feet.

'Has new idea,' Fodur panted. 'I comes with you.'

'Good. Can you run?'

'Fast, fast,' Fodur confirmed.

'Stay close. We don't have long.'

Sylvan shoved his way past Fodur and back out into the tunnel. This was a Singer's burrow. This tunnel would lead to a higher one, and then to a feeding hole. But they had to get there before the water. Sylvan set off, splashing down the passage. He could hear Fodur behind as they half ran, half waded, battered by rushes of water. The darkness was absolute. Their only guides were Sylvan's whiskers and his instinct for the turns of the burrow. They moved quickly, gaining height and turning corners. But even as they raced, the water swirled around their feet, then their thighs and their bellies. It was climbing faster than they were. Even as he thought it, the earth beneath Sylvan's paws disappeared and dropped into a deep pool. He scrabbled backwards so fast that Fodur collided with him.

'What's it?'

'Water. The tunnel dips. We'll have to swim.'

'Swim?' Fodur was appalled.

'No choice. Come on.'

Sylvan cast himself into the water, paddling strongly. After a moment he felt something at his heels. Fodur. The rat had followed, thank Sinethis. Sylvan forged ahead. The earth ceiling scraped along Sylvan's spine as he swam. The air now was nothing but a thin layer at the very top of the tunnel. He had to raise his nose to breathe. A wave raced up behind, washing under and over him. Sylvan was forced under as the water swelled. He spluttered to the surface. A moment of claustrophobic panic, fought down. A quick check: Fodur was still behind. He swam on. Abruptly his nose banged against earth. He stopped dead, then dived down, seeking the path ahead. Momentary relief. The tunnel was not blocked. But it had dipped below the water's surface, and, he realized, was filled to the top. No air. He twisted round and retreated. He resurfaced in the thin layer of air just as Fodur pulled alongside. The rat's breathing was ragged. Sylvan could hear it whistle as Fodur held his nose to the ceiling.

'Bad news, Fodur,' Sylvan gasped. 'The tunnel goes down.'

Their bodies bobbed together in the dark. Sylvan drew in a breath. The water lapped higher. If it came up further the air space would soon be gone.

'Bad for rats,' panted Fodur. 'What we do?'

'We need to dive. The tunnel's filled. But it won't be far,' said Sylvan.

'Dive? No. Needs to go back.'

'There is no "back",' said Sylvan. 'It's underwater. It's gone.'

Another surge piled over their heads, thrusting the pair of them down. Sylvan pulled for the ceiling, praying the air would still be there. His muzzle broke out of the water. Thank Sinethis. But another wave could finish them.

'Tunnel's short. Dive, Fodur. Go first. I'll help.'

'Not good for—'

More water flooded. They surfaced choking and coughing. The air was noticeably thinner now.

'I don't care what it's good for,' Sylvan shouted. 'If you want to live, you dive.'

'But—'

'Do it!'

Fodur hesitated. A swirl of water and Sylvan's mouth and nose were filled. He spat the liquid out.

'Dive!' he yelled.

Fodur dragged in a rasping breath and shoved himself downwards, barging past Sylvan and on down the flooded tunnel. Sylvan followed, diving cleanly. The only sound now was the rush and bubble of water. Sylvan's whiskers brushed something. Wall. Follow. His paws scraped the tunnel floor, gained purchase. He shoved hard and his back smacked against the roof. He lifted his nose. No air. He reached out and dragged at the walls, thrusting himself forwards. He paddled, kicked, and scraped at any surface he could reach. Anything to get him down the tunnel. Fodur's tail whisked past Sylvan's face and Sylvan felt the wash from Fodur's good back leg as it churned the water in front of him. He pulled back to give Fodur room. But every instinct screamed at him to go faster. He raised his nose again. Only water. A knot formed in his belly. They were only going to be able to hold their breath for so long. The tunnel had to rise soon. Sylvan made two swift strokes, reached out, and shoved at Fodur with his forepaws, urging him on. Even as he did it, he felt his chest begin to tighten: the seed of a need to breathe. The tunnel must end. It must.

Fodur stopped dead. He started to lash out with his paws, as if fighting something unseen in the water ahead. Sylvan shoved past him—and swam straight into slick mud. It blocked the tunnel, solid to the roof. Impassable. Even as horror gripped him, Sylvan's paws were searching for where the mud joined the ceiling. He found the place, and began to scrape and chew at it, his paws joining Fodur's. He raked back great clods that thickened the water behind them. The urge to breathe rose up, but he dared not give in. This was their only hope, to clear the tunnel, to get past. A sick need grew in his lungs. He clawed feverishly at the soil and stones, hurling them aside. But the wall held.

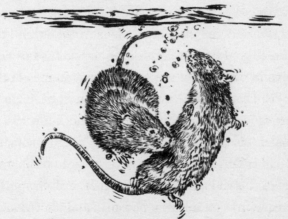

Forced beyond endurance, Sylvan let go his stock of air. Bubbles rose around him. A momentary relief, quickly gone. And now his empty lungs must be filled. His gut muscles clenched, trying to pull air into his closed nostrils. He lashed at the earth begging it to give. He cursed Sinethis in his mind, hurling words at her in a fury of bitterness. *Why? You drove me from my home. Why? So you could drown me?*

And Sinethis tore into him with a wordless scream of rage. Blackness welled up as he filled with her turmoil. Sylvan fought her, shutting her from his mind, silently yelling his defiance. And with a final gigantic heave he hurled himself kicking and battling at the mud wall. His guts, lungs and throat screamed at him. He thrashed. No air. Water. No air.

Then the earth gave. Mud cascaded. Sylvan scrabbled for purchase, found a grip. He thrust down, and smashed through into air. He gulped down a breath of mixed air, mud, and water. He hacked and coughed and swam in the pitch-blackness. Safe. Breathing. But no Fodur. The rat had not come up. He had been beside Sylvan under the water, digging at the same earth. Why hadn't he come up? Sylvan gasped down another lungful, ignoring his body's protests, and knifed back down into the tunnel. His paws found something that flinched from his touch. Fodur. He threw his forelegs around the rat's body and heaved backwards. Nothing gave. Another heave and Fodur came free in a flurry of flailing claws. Sylvan tugged him out of the mud and up through the water to the surface.

Blackness, filled with the sound of coughing and panting. Sylvan, chest heaving, sick to his stomach, paddled the water, with barely the strength to keep himself afloat. His whiskers brushed the wall to his right. To his left he sensed Fodur. The rat too was breathing heavily, but swimming. Beyond the thick walls of the riverbank was the muted roar of Sinethis. Sylvan had never heard anything like it in his life. Sinethis was everywhere, snarling and swirling at the level of their heads, separated from them by only the thin earth wall. The sound terrified him.

Fodur's body bumped gently against Sylvan's flank as the water swelled around them.

'Heh,' Fodur panted. 'We's alive, then.'

'Looks . . . like it.'

'Is good . . . Fodur likes breathing.'

Something like a laugh spluttered out of Sylvan's mouth, causing him to inhale more mud. He coughed it out and a swell lifted him until the fur of his back brushed against the earth ceiling. He paddled forwards a little, to where he sensed the roof was higher. His whiskers touched the far wall. The whole space was no more than two Singers' lengths across.

'Has a . . . question,' said Fodur.

'What question?'

'Where is we?'

'The tunnel collapsed,' said Sylvan. 'Soil fell from the roof. We're where the soil came from.'

'Ah.' Fodur was silent for some moments. 'We's in water above the tunnel?'

'Yes.'

'This is not being good.'

'No,' said Sylvan. 'It's bad.'

'Glad we agrees.'

Sylvan's back nudged against the ceiling again. He tried to swim forwards, but still soil brushed against him. The space above them had got smaller.

'Fodur,' said Sylvan, 'the water's still rising.'

Splashing and scraping as Fodur felt his way around.

'You's right. Your Sinethis not be liking us.'

'She doesn't *like* anyone,' Sylvan snapped. 'Now think of a way out of here.'

Fresh panic. Sylvan's mind raced. The water would squeeze the air out of this space, just as it had below. The burrow below was filled. If they dived back into the tunnel . . . he shuddered. They couldn't go back. He listened to the Great River rampaging down her course. She was pressing her waters up from below, shoving their backs against the ceiling. She was squeezing them to death. Anger stirred in him. *Right*, Sylvan thought. *If you want a fight, Sinethis, I'll give you one.*

'Dig,' said Sylvan. 'We've got to dig.'

'Sylvan, I—'

'I said *dig*,' Sylvan shouted. 'Up. We're at the top of the burrow. We need a feeding hole.'

Sylvan reached above his head, letting his hind feet drop down into the water. He began to scrape at the ceiling, paddling with his hind legs to keep himself afloat. He could hear Fodur beside him, struggling vainly with his one good leg. Soil rained from the roof onto his head, clogging his nostrils and forcing his eyes shut. Already tired, Sylvan's muscles burned with fatigue. It was impossible. Sylvan kept his paws up as long as he could, but pushed to his limits he gave in. He sank back into the water, letting himself bob on the surface.

'It's no good,' Sylvan gasped. 'I can't do it. Sorry.'

The water lapped around the two friends, pressing them upwards.

'I tried, Sinethis,' said Sylvan bitterly. 'I fought you. If you're going to take us, take us. But I know that I fought.'

'Heh,' said Fodur. 'Fight, fight. Is nothing else for Sinethis?'

'No,' said Sylvan.

'Is shame,' said Fodur. 'Let me tells you how it is for rats.' His voice was odd. He sounded calm, now, speaking almost conversationally. Didn't he know they were going to die here? 'We has Mother, Hunter, Trickster, and Taker. We loves the Mother, runs with the Hunter, and dances with the Trickster.'

Sylvan said nothing. A swell passed between them, flowing across his muzzle. *Not long*, he thought.

'Dance well, run well, love well and you's most of a rat.' Fodur continued. 'But the Taker he comes unseen and alone.

To be the whole rat, you keeps yourself ready for him. You sees?'

'No,' said Sylvan. 'I don't understand.'

It was an effort, now, to keep his head up. His back fur filled with soil from where it rubbed the ceiling. More water had entered. More air had gone. And he and Fodur were talking. But then, thought Sylvan, what else could they do?

'The Hunter and Trickster, they twists us like your Sinethis. But the Taker is beyond them. He you do not fight. You keeps a place in yourself. You keeps ready.'

And Sylvan thought he understood. He had fought all his life, enemies or Sinethis. It had not mattered. You fought and you lived. But there was something in Fodur's words that made sense. Perhaps some things you could not fight. Perhaps giving in was right, at the right time.

'Are you?' asked Sylvan. 'Ready I mean?'

'Heh. I's old,' said Fodur. 'Has been ready for long time. The Taker comes quiet, and brings us to his land beyond. We be happy there, methinks.'

Sylvan raised his head. He could barely keep his mouth clear.

'Fodur,' said Sylvan. Water trickled into his mouth. He spat it out. 'It's been a privilege to know you.'

Sylvan felt a paw against his beneath the water. He grasped it, tightly.

'The same,' said Fodur.

Water splashed into Sylvan's nostrils. He angled his body so that his nose had more room. His mouth was below the surface, now, and he could not speak. But then he had nothing more to say. Sinethis would fill the space and take his life. Sylvan wondered if it would hurt.

Strife paused for long enough to slough the mud from her paws and wipe the water from her eyes. She glared up at the rain, then back down at the banktop beneath her paws. Her sides heaved with effort. Kale spat out a mouthful of liquid mud and raised his head.

'Keep digging.'

'I *am* digging, Kale,' said Strife. She returned to work. 'I just don't know *why* I'm digging.'

'Just do it. Trust me.'

'Trust you? Hah!' Strife pawed aside a clump of grass and rolled it into the river. 'I'm never going to trust you again.'

'Fine. Whatever. Just dig, as fast as you can.'

Strife dug, using her teeth to chew down into the bank. She had no idea why Kale had chosen this spot, but she had to do something. She was soaked to the skin, cold and frightened. She was standing with her brother, up to her neck in a muddy hole that they were excavating in the riverbank. *Hah*, she thought. *Kale is up to his neck in it in more ways than one.*

But Kale had got her out of the burrow. Strife had woken with his paw shaking her and he had led her, dazed, sleepy, and complaining, through the tunnels and out onto the riverbank. And even as their paws met the grass, Sinethis had surged upwards, grasping and reaching as if she wanted to smother the whole of the land. Strife had run back to the burrow entrance, thinking to go back in, find the others. But Kale, moving faster than she thought he could, had blocked her path, dragged her away.

Not that way, he had said. *She'll drown you.* He released his grip on her. *There's another way.*

And this was his other way. Rain splashed down, filling their hole with filthy water. Behind them was the Great River, her waters swift and bulging. Sinethis raced past the banktop

and bubbled up through the feeding holes. Everything else—
the platforms, the entrances, the bank itself, all of it—was
gone. All they had was the banktop and fields. And the
digging. Strife's shoulders, jaw, and back ached with the
effort. But she kept going because Kale told her to. Because
his certainty gave her hope.

Strife's head came up again, and again she cleaned the
mud from her muzzle. The river was almost level with them.
If Sylvan and Fodur were inside, then surely Sinethis would
have taken them by now. But no, she could not think that.
While Kale had hope, so did she. She lowered her muzzle
and opened her mouth, bracing with a paw—

—which went straight through the ground, causing her
to topple forwards. Kale grabbed her scruff and yanked
her away. Together they scrabbled free in time to see the
remaining soil tumbling down into a hole. For a moment
Strife thought that the whole bank had gone, that the river
had carved off a chunk of land. But Kale dashed to the edge,
shouting words of encouragement. A pair of paws appeared,
followed by a bedraggled, mud-smeared, pointy face. Strife
blinked. And a feeling of joyful disbelief spread through her.

'Uncle Fodur!'

It was Fodur. He pawed at the edge, splashing in the water. From down in the hole, Sylvan's voice yelled a complaint. In an instant Strife had bounded to her feet and dashed forwards, barging past Kale and nearly sliding into the pit in her enthusiasm. She peered down at the top of Sylvan's head. He swam grimly in thick mud; plastered and exhausted but alive. She felt a grin of sheer delight on her face. Her uncles were alive!

'Missy Strife?'

'Yes, Uncle Fodur?'

Next to her Fodur had both front elbows hooked over the lip of the hole, and his chest was heaving.

'Is . . . chance you could be helping?'

'Ooh, sorry. Of course. Come on, Kale.'

The pair of them took hold of Fodur's fur and tugged him up the bank. The rain and soil made it difficult, but eventually

Fodur pitched forwards out of the hole, landing flat on the mud. Strife fell backwards and clambered to her feet.

'Sylvan?' she called. 'Are you OK?'

Sylvan's paws appeared at the lip of the hole. It took him several attempts to haul up enough to lay his head on what was left of the grass. He gave a short hacking sound that might have been a laugh.

'Oh, just great. Never better.' He raised his head and shouted, 'You hear that, Sinethis? I said I'm never better. So next time you try to drown me you'd better try harder.'

He coughed again, nearly slipping back into the quagmire. He got his elbows over the edge and hung on his forelegs, the rest of him dangling in liquid mud. It looked very odd to see a disembodied Singer's head poking up out of the ground. Strife would have laughed, but judging by Sylvan's ferocious expression he wouldn't have taken it well.

Strife leant towards Fodur, who was still lying on his side, enjoying the air. She dropped her voice to a discreet whisper.

'Um, is Uncle Sylvan all right?'

'Is OK. Is upset with your Sinethis, is all.' Fodur managed a weak smile. 'I knows the feeling.'

'And don't worry about me,' called Sylvan bitterly. 'You just carry on with your conversation. I'm sure I'll be able to hack my way out of this pit eventually.'

'He's definitely all right,' said Strife to Kale. She moved

closer to the hole. 'He's not very grateful, though.' She looked disapprovingly down at Sylvan. 'If I had just been rescued by a pair of brave young River Singers, I wouldn't be nasty to them.'

'Strife—' Sylvan began with a warning note. But she was on a roll.

'You know,' Strife said, 'if two wonderful and under-appreciated Singers had just saved *me* from drowning, I'd be *really* nice to them. In fact,' she continued, 'I'd be thinking about some of the horrid things that I'd said in the past and probably be feeling quite regretful. I might even want to apologize.' She pattered a little closer to where Sylvan glowered up at her. 'Do you feel at all like that?' she asked. 'Like you want to say sorry for anything?'

Sylvan scowled. 'No,' he said. 'I don't. Do you?'

His fur was plastered to his body. Mud dripped off him in all directions and his whiskers drooped wetly. Above these his glare was furious. The effect was utterly ridiculous. Strife started to giggle. She tried to resist but could not control it. It was the expression on his face that did it. She put both paws over her mouth, but the laughter forced its way out. She sat down in the mud and let it come.

Sylvan's scowl gradually faded, replaced by a look of weary resignation. He rested his chin on his paws and waited for Strife to stop. Eventually she sobered.

'Strife,' said Sylvan, 'has anyone ever told you that you're one of the most irritating River Singers who has ever lived?'

'Oh, yes. Quite often.'

'Good. Just so long as you know.' Then Sylvan let go a breath and gave her a lopsided smile. 'But you're right. You saved my life. And Fodur's life. And I'm sorry for being ungrateful. Thank you.'

Strife regarded him solemnly. 'You're welcome,' she said. She stood up. 'Would you like help getting out of that hole?'

'Yes, please.'

Water lapped coldly around Strife's feet. She glanced down in surprise. She had thought she was on the banktop. But now her feet were wet. Kale gave a single warning shout, pointing upflow. Strife's head snapped up to see . . . nothing. Upflow was gone. In its place a churning wall of greyish water hurtled towards them. Snatched images: water pouring into the hole, Sylvan thrashing in mud, water roiling, bubbles, foam. And Strife was smashed aside by an incredible force as Sinethis rolled into and over her, obliterating everything. Head and ears ringing. Cold. Swirling.

Strife surfaced, gasping with shock. She shook her head clear of the water. She saw Uncle Fodur scrambling up the bank, Sylvan swimming towards her, Kale diving for the river. Then Sinethis took her, yanking her from the shallows and pitching her into the turmoil of the main flow. Something collided with Strife, spinning her around. A floating branch. She tried to shove free of it, but a wave went over her. She spluttered up and faced the bank. She was being borne away from the land. She swam for the bank, but even so it slipped further away. Wave after wave slammed against her body. Then the branch hit her once more, nudging her downstream. She lashed out at it, and her body pivoted so that her nose was in line with Sinethis's flow.

And the assault stopped instantly. Her swimming became smooth, powerful. Around Strife rolling walls of angry, brown water raced downflow, but now she moved with them. Ahead she could make out the tiny form of a Singer. Kale. He too was swimming downflow, drawing further from her with each passing moment.

'Kale!'

He did not respond, either unable to hear, or not caring. She kicked after him. She rode Sinethis's flow, using her legs and paws to hold the Great River at bay. She surfed the currents, applying her strength where it was needed,

fighting the battles, keeping her balance. Ahead, Kale almost seemed to dance in the water, now rolling across a thick rope of current, now cutting into an eddy, snatching a breath, then spilling diagonally into a valley and forging up the other side.

'Kale! Get to the side!'

But still he did not hear her. And instead of heading for the bank he made for the centre where the torrent was fastest. She could not imagine what he was doing. Lost among the rush and struggle Strife could only hang on and follow as closely as she dared. She kept her eyes locked on his tiny form as he bobbed and ducked amidst the swells. The bank flew past, faster than she could have believed, tilting crazily. Part of Strife's mind shouted that she must get out, that she was tired and Sinethis could kill her. But she would not stop without Kale. She hurtled, barely surviving, down the Great River. And still Kale did not swim for the shore.

Strife yelled her brother's name. She swam until her shoulders ached and her breath came in sobs. A surge crashed against her, rocking her to the side. She tried to shove against it, but missed her stroke. Her body spun in the current and Sinethis powered into her. Strife pitched over and Sinethis thrust her down. She scrambled up to the air with short, panicked strokes. Her ears rang with a cold frenzy. The sound filled Strife with deadly certainty. The ducking had been a warning: Sinethis had been playing with her, but the game was over. If she carried on after her brother, Sinethis would kill her.

'Kale, p-please . . .'

But her voice went unheeded. Ahead, the main current

was flanked by calm waters. Kale, though, looked neither left nor right, but swam on down the flow. Strife made one last attempt to follow. But before she could even try, the Great River rang louder in her ears and swells smashed against her.

'All right,' Strife gasped. 'You win.'

And now she could not follow where Kale led. She cried out with the bitterest sense of loss she had ever known. Then she turned for the bank. The roar died and the waters calmed around her. She found a place where the flow eddied back behind a fallen tree. She paddled to the shore, sobbing with mixed exhaustion and grief. Strife dragged herself from the water and crept into a clump of grass. She stared downflow with eyes that blurred and cleared as she blinked. Of Kale there was no sign. Sinethis had carried him away. And she had left Strife cold and alone, shivering on her banks.

Strife watched the land grasses as they waved beneath their fresh coating of water. There was something helpless about these drowned plants. Sinethis had smothered them, snapped them, and forced them to bow their heads. She had invaded their world as if she had every right to be there. But this was not Sinethis's place. She should not have done this. From in front of Strife the new shallows lapped delicately at the banktop, as if tasting it. And beyond those shallows the torrent thundered, filling every other space with sound. The Great River stretched out in a turbid roiling expanse from Strife's toes to the very edge of the fields. And the fields continued away flatly, to be lost in the distance. The same fields lay behind Strife. She kept her back to them. As terrible as the Great River was, she was far, far better than that yawning plain of grass. Strife could see no cows, or animals of any sort. That, at least, was a relief. But neither could she see any sign of the woods they had come through. Or any food, or shelter.

And there was precious little shelter, now, even on the riverbanks. The banks, and all of their plants, were gone. Strife had been born in a burrow, surrounded by tall herbs and grasses. She had thought that these things were eternal, like the air she breathed. Oh, there were enemies, but you could run and you could fight. You could dive or hide. But now her world had been revealed as nothing but a fragile ribbon, squeezed between the water and the land. Sinethis had destroyed it easily, leaving only this strip, no wider than a Singer. Nothing was left for Strife. Not Uncle Fodur, not Sylvan, not Kale. Tears stung in her eyes, threatening to leak out and down her face. But she forced them back. *I won't cry*, she thought. *There's enough water in the world without me adding to it. You hear me Sinethis? You won't make me cry.*

A crack of a twig. Silence. Strife lifted her head. A small

noise, quickly stifled. Something was moving through the grasses. An enemy. Strife climbed to her feet, ready to dive. It was so strange. Sinethis had carried her brother away and could take her life in an instant. But still she remained Strife's only escape. As Strife listened for more sounds, she glared down at the water. *Don't think that just because I need you this makes us even. It doesn't. The other Singers might be your children, but you're no mother to me.* To her right a soft crashing. She tensed. More sounds. A snatch of something, whisked from audibility by the wind. A scatter of words, spoken in low voices.

' . . . is close by, methinks. Is her smell ahead.'

'I hope you're right.'

'Tsk. You should be trusting the nose.'

'I *do* trust the nose, Fodur.' Sylvan's voice, sounding weary. 'I've just had enough surprises today, that's all.'

Strife sagged with relief. Then the grasses parted and Sylvan staggered to a stop in front of her. He focused on her face.

'Strife,' he said, as if unsure that it was really her. Then he stumbled around in a circle and called back, 'Fodur. It's OK. She's here.'

A strange mixture of feelings: joy that her uncles were with her, the aching loss of Kale, anger at Sinethis. It threatened to overwhelm her. Tears pricked her eyes, but again she forced them away. She reached for the hard place that had made her follow Kale; that had made her fight. She surveyed the state of her uncle for some moments.

'You look terrible.'

'Thanks,' said Sylvan. He gave her a tired smile. 'It's good to see you too. Where's Kale?'

'Gone,' she said shortly. 'Sinethis carried him away and he swam off.' She gestured with her chin. 'That way.'

'Ah,' said Sylvan. 'Did he, now.'

For a moment Strife thought she saw a glint in his eye, but then his head dropped.

'I'm tired,' he mumbled. He turned himself round in the small space, moving stiffly, to watch for Fodur. After a few moments the rat's sharp nose parted the grasses, and he hobbled into the clump.

'Missy Strife,' he said happily. 'We finds you.'

Strife rolled her eyes. For some reason they both seemed intent on stating the obvious.

'Yes, it's me,' said Strife impatiently. 'Strife.' Seeing his hurt look she added, 'And I'm so glad to see you, of course, Uncle Fodur. But we've got to go. Sinethis took Kale away. He could be in trouble or anything.'

Sylvan groaned and sat down heavily. Fodur slumped next to him.

'I'm sorry, Strife,' said Sylvan. 'I can't. We have to rest.'

'Is right,' said Fodur. 'I's a done rat.'

'But—' Strife began.

Sylvan raised his head with an effort. It nodded slightly as he spoke.

'Strife,' he said. 'I know how you feel. You want to get after Kale. I feel the same. But we've had a bad time of things. We need to sleep and we need to eat. If we carry on as we are we'll be taken by an enemy. I'm sorry.' Sylvan gave her a sympathetic smile. 'We'll go later, I promise.'

Then Sylvan shuffled deeper into the tuft and curled up. Fodur followed, with an apologetic look. Strife filled with bitter disappointment. Kale could be hurt. Didn't they care? But then she realized she was being unfair. Despite everything a small smile tugged at the edges of her mouth. Her uncles were safe. They had come all this way to find her. They had nearly drowned, and still they had walked down the river. All for her. They might be exhausted now, but she knew they wouldn't stop until they found Kale. She just needed to be patient.

Strife settled down to watch over them. Apart from the rush of the water, and the occasional snore from Uncle Fodur, things were calm. The sky was flat grey and the rain had given way to a fitful drizzle. She saw no enemies. From time to time she grazed. The whole world seemed subdued, as if the events of the morning had shocked it to quietness.

Eventually a movement behind Strife announced that Sylvan had woken. He staggered from his makeshift nest, looking rumpled but more rested. Then he settled next to her and grabbed for a pawful of land grasses. He munched them hungrily.

'Done sleeping?' she said.

'Huh,' said Sylvan past his mouthful. 'Only because Fodur started snoring. I thought I'd take my chances out here.'

Strife smiled. 'Yes, he's loud, isn't he? We used to be able to hear him all over the burrow. Mother said that it was

useful for keeping the enemies away.' She turned back to look over the water. 'I like the sound. It makes me feel safe.'

'I don't. It gives me earache.'

Sylvan wolfed down some more grasses. Then he groomed his whiskers and straightened his fur. When he was done he nodded at the river.

'Looks odd, doesn't she?'

'Odd?' said Strife. 'Who looks odd?'

'Sinethis.'

What on earth was he talking about?

'You call this *odd*?' Sylvan was obviously a master of understatement. 'You do know that Sinethis tried to kill us, don't you? And she's got Kale. And it's all gone. There are no burrows, no shelter, nothing. We're stuck here on her banks and far from home and—'

'Exactly,' Sylvan interrupted. 'If all that isn't odd I don't know what is.'

Strife stared at him. 'What's wrong with you? Aren't you even upset?'

'Of course I'm upset,' said Sylvan. 'I'm very upset. But upset is normal when you're dealing with Sinethis. Besides, I think you're wrong.'

'What about?'

'Sinethis. She didn't try to kill us. If she had tried, she'd have done it, believe me. She was testing.'

'Testing what? How much a River Singer enjoys being hit by a massive wall of water and seeing her brother swept away? It's not much, I can tell you.' Strife scowled at the water. 'If that's her idea of a test I'd hate to see what she does when she's really got it in for you.'

Sylvan scratched distractedly at a patch of dried mud that had clumped in his fur. 'No, that wave wasn't much fun, I agree. But it might have been my fault a bit.'

'Oh, come on,' Strife scoffed. 'That's completely stupid. How can it possibly be your fault? It's not like you asked her to do that, is it?'

'I taunted her,' said Sylvan. 'Sinethis takes things like that personally.'

Strife's eyes narrowed. 'You talk as though Sinethis is a person. Like when you said to Mother that Sinethis was calling you or something.'

Sylvan nodded. 'Yes. She does speak to me, sometimes. Usually to make me fight or do something I don't want to. Other times it's just a feeling.' He shrugged. 'That I need to go somewhere or do something. I've learned to listen to that.' He gave her a meaningful look. 'And I think Kale has too.'

Strife stared at him.

'I think that Sinethis has something planned for him,' Sylvan continued. 'She called him. That's why he left and that's why he's gone ahead.'

Strife wanted to laugh, to dismiss the idea. But it fitted too well with what Kale had said and the turns he had taken, the things he had seemed to know. And she remembered the light across the water when she had prayed for safety from the owl. She remembered how the Great River had poured into her thoughts after her escape from the cows.

She had spoken to Sinethis, and the noise had stopped. She remembered the way Sinethis had rung in her ears and forced her not to follow Kale. And suddenly Strife felt small, and afraid.

'Oh,' she said. She gazed at the pounding river. 'She's really real, then.'

'Yes, I'm afraid so,' said Sylvan. 'And at the moment she's not very happy about something. But she kept us alive. That's usually a good sign.'

Strife's head came up. 'Alive for what?' she asked sharply.

'Sinethis likes us to fight,' said Sylvan. He sighed. 'We live as sacrifice and that's what she demands. Follow her and fight her. Do both hard enough and she'll give you what you want. That's the bargain.'

'And what if you don't want to be a sacrifice?' said Strife. 'What if you don't fight?'

Sylvan pulled a face. But he was spared answering by Fodur limping into view. The rat cocked his head.

'Ready is we?'

'Oh, yes. Ready for the fight, as ever,' said Sylvan, catching Strife's eye. 'We should get after Kale. I don't think he'll be too far.'

That sounded a little too certain for Strife. 'Are you guessing, or do you know something?' she demanded.

Sylvan smiled. 'I've got a feeling,' he said. 'Good enough?'

Strife let go a breath. 'It'll do. But I want it to be known that I'm not at all happy about this.'

'I'm sure Sinethis will take that into consideration. Coming?'

Without waiting for a response, Sylvan led off through the grasses. He skirted the waters and headed downflow. Strife looked at Fodur who merely flicked an ear and set off after Sylvan. Strife watched them go. She wasn't at all sure how she felt about Singers who talked to Sinethis. It sounded strange and frightening at the same time. Then she scampered after the others. Sinethis or no Sinethis, she had a brother to find. And after that, she thought, she was getting back to the Wetted Land just as fast as she could.

PART 3
THE RETURN

'Tell me why you came here.'

The female stopped watching the water and fastened her gaze on Kale. Her scrutiny made him uncomfortable. She had a way of looking at him that seemed to be assessing him down to his bones. She had the look of a Singer who knew about the world. And the knowledge had made her hard.

'But I told you, Mistress' he said.

'Actually you didn't.' She spoke mildly, but her words had a stony quality to them. 'You only told me *how* you came here. You said you left this Wetted Land of yours, came to the Great River, and were swept away. That I understand. But I'm more interested in *why* you did these things. Why leave your home?'

Her way of questioning left Kale completely wrong-footed. This was the place he was meant to be, of that he was certain. But the compulsion that had driven him was gone. It had brought him to this place and abandoned him. The water had washed him up to this bare earth hollow beneath its meagre tangle of tree roots and grass. And this Singer had already been here. Even if she had not actually been waiting for him, she had shown no surprise at his arrival. She was a puzzle. She had an air of calm and self-assurance, but it was shallow, somehow. As if beneath the surface all of her softness had gone, leaving her stony and brittle.

'Because of Sinethis, Mistress,' he answered. 'She brought me here. I don't know why, though.'

He told her the truth. He had no other option. Lying to this female probably wouldn't get him very far. He watched her carefully and to his surprise her features twisted into a tight smile.

'Ah,' she said. 'Sinethis. Just going with the flow, were you? How nice.' She turned back to the river. 'I've heard Singers say that they were following Sinethis. Never very many, and they never stop anywhere for long. I even did it myself, once.' Her brows drew together. 'Those that follow always have somewhere else to be. They pass through and away. And you never discover what happens to them.'

Then she gave him an amused look. 'And here you are. My

chance to find out, it appears. You'd never seen your Sinethis before? You didn't know what she was capable of?'

'No, Mistress.'

'I thought not.'

The amusement vanished. After a moment the female gestured at the water as it ran below her paws. 'Well, follower of Sinethis, let me show you something. Come and have a look in the water here. Tell me what you see.'

Kale hesitated. He took a few uncertain steps and stopped. He felt bashful and, if he was honest, a little afraid. She made an impatient gesture.

'Oh, come on. I won't bite you.'

She moved aside to make room beside her on the muddy ledge. As she moved he caught sight of her tail. It whipped quickly from view, but not before he noticed, with a slightly sick feeling, that half of it was missing. He pulled his gaze away and joined her on the ledge. Her face clearly said that she had noticed his reaction. She did not comment, though.

'Do you have any idea what's down there?' she asked.

Kale peered into the depths. He could see nothing but murky water.

'I know. It's a bit of an unfair question. There's no reason you should, really. After all you've only just arrived. But you seem like an intelligent vole, so maybe you can have a guess.'

Kale blinked and did not answer. Keeping quiet was

usually the best option. And something in her tone told him that a response would not be welcome.

'Well, I'll tell you,' she said. 'That's my home down there. Under the water. And not only mine. There were many of us.' Her voice remained steady but her whiskers quivered as she spoke. 'Oh, not as many as there could have been. The mink saw to that. But enough for a life. Until Sinethis took them.'

She turned her head and regarded Kale solemnly. 'I waited here long after it grew light, and all morning. I've seen no others apart from you. Maybe they survived and were swept along with the water as you were. Or more likely Sinethis caught them in their burrows and took them. I don't know. But one way or another they're gone.'

She lapsed into silence and fixed him with her uncomfortable gaze. Kale felt that he should say something, or do something to make things better. There was nothing he could think of. But still he found words in his mouth, and heard them pass his lips.

'Did you . . . erm . . . have . . . '

'What?'

'Children.'

'Pups?' She gave a short laugh, more of a bark. 'No, thankfully. I had enough reason to fear Sinethis before this. I had no wish to bring any new Singers into this world.'

And that, thought Kale, is what you get for speaking. He closed his mouth firmly and they sat together in silence for a long while.

'So,' said the female at last. 'Why do you think the Great River was so determined for us to meet?'

'I don't know.'

'That's a shame. I could have done with some hope.'

Kale settled down on the ledge, wondering what happened now. This was not what he had been expecting. Sinethis had led and he had followed. And now, as though she had no further use for him, she had gone.

'Any idea what we do now?' inquired the female.

'We wait,' said Kale.

The female burst out laughing. Kale watched her closely. The laughter seemed genuine, but it had a bitter edge to it.

'Sorry, Mistress, but what's funny?'

'Oh, nothing really. It just struck me that way.' She lowered her head onto her forepaws. 'So I'll wait here with you. It's not like I had anything better to do today.'

Together they watched the slow creep of water up towards their ledge. When one of them grew hungry they nibbled at the tufts of grass that grew between the interlacing roots. Rain showers passed, but only a few drops from a whiteish sky. And so they waited and watched as the afternoon drifted silently towards evening.

'Ready? Go.'

Strife and Fodur dashed across the short grass of the field. They skirted the water and dived for the rushes. A rustle and they were gone. Sylvan eyed the distance to the stand. Longer than he would like, but nothing to be done. He crouched, then launched himself after them, following an arcing path along the water's edge. To Sylvan's left the grasses stretched up an increasingly steep incline to a dark line of hilltop woods. To his right they glistened beneath a film of water. The Great River now formed the deeper heart of a wide, shallow lake, one that moment by moment oozed further across the

low-lying lands. Sylvan's foot splashed into a small dip and he adjusted his course. He sprinted as fast as he could. But with every step the itch between his shoulders and the naked feeling of exposure grew. He risked a glance around. No birds, no land predators. Thank Sinethis. And then he was diving into the meagre embrace of the rushes, breath coming hard. Strife and Fodur were there, staring at the path ahead.

'How much further is it now?' asked Strife.

'For the last time, I don't know,' panted Sylvan. 'Stop asking.'

He was probably being too hard on her. This field was interminable. And it held nothing for a Singer but death. Its grasses were so short that two voles and a rat running down the water's edge were clearly visible for any predator that cared to look. Worse, the river's course was increasingly difficult to follow. No longer constrained by her banks, Sinethis filled all of the land's rucks and hollows, pushing deeply into the fields. Here and there higher sections of bank and lone trees poked up like islands. But around these the waters swirled deceptively. For the River Singers these islands offered an escape from the land enemies, but Fodur could not swim as

they could. And so for his sake they skirted the water when possible, following the Great River's now unclear course as it curved around the hill.

'I'm tired,' Strife complained, 'and I feel like I'm going to be taken any moment.'

Sylvan's lips tightened. He couldn't see what she expected him to do about it.

'I thought you wanted to find Kale?'

'I do,' she said. 'But there's not much point finding him if we're already dead, now, is there?'

'All right,' said Sylvan. 'So what do *you* think we should do?'

Strife pointed with her chin at a jutting piece of bank with a tree growing from it. It was a short swim away, through calm-looking floodwater.

'I say we head for that and stay there overnight. Then we find Kale tomorrow.'

Fodur nodded slowly in agreement. Sylvan took in the lengthening shadows, and felt the heaviness in his muscles that his brief sleep had not dispelled. The lone island did look inviting. And anything had to be better than this field.

'You know what?' he said. 'For once that was actually a sensible suggestion. Well done.'

Strife gave him a haughty look, tinged with just a hint of pride.

'Not everything I say is stupid, you know.'

'So you keep telling me. Right, let's go for it. Strife, you lead the way.'

Strife nodded once and then briefly scented the air before slipping from the rushes into the water. She half waded, half paddled into the broad lake, and was soon swimming towards the island. She met the current as it cut around behind the tree, angling her body to counteract it. She reached the shore and pulled herself cautiously from the water, sniffing all around for scents of danger. Then she rose half way on her haunches and raised a paw before disappearing into the thicker grasses.

'You know,' said Sylvan, impressed, 'there's just a possibility that she might make a decent Singer one day.'

'I always thinks that Missy Strife is one of best,' said Fodur. 'I's glad you sees it.'

'I'd have seen it a lot quicker if she was less irritating.'

Sylvan slid into the water with Fodur trailing. He swam quickly to limit the time he spent in the river's cold embrace. When Sylvan reached the island and had shaken himself dry Fodur was still swimming. Sylvan checked for predators and settled down to watch, ready to step in if the current looked like carrying his friend away.

From behind the tree came a terrible, high-pitched scream. Sylvan was on his feet in an instant, racing toward the sound. He parted the grasses at the top and stared down through the tangled roots, seeking the source of the noise. His view filled with a wittering ball of angry enthusiasm. Strife was jumping up and down and shrieking at the top of her voice. He could barely hear the words, but they seemed to be conveying a mixture of joy and extreme outrage. In front of Strife, staggering away from the onslaught, was Kale. Sylvan grinned. Kale almost got beyond reach before Strife grabbed him and yanked him forwards. Then she pummelled him with her paws. When he raised his own paws to ward off the attack Strife switched tactics by speeding up the flow of words.

' . . . believe you went off like that, I mean what were you thinking, you could have been killed or anything and we were so worried and you're a complete moron, and I'm really not happy with you . . . '

Sylvan's attention slipped to Kale's companion who had shrunk back against a tree root, teeth half-bared. A female River Singer. And one who looked achingly familiar. The grin fell from his face.

' . . . ever do anything like that again I'll completely kill you, well I won't kill you, but I'll think of something that will definitely make you wish I *had* killed you, and then I'll do whatever it was that I thought of a lot more, and then . . . '

Sylvan's jaw dropped open. The female looked up at him. She came fully up on her haunches, paws raised, ears flat. She looked as though she had been struck, or as though she might attack. Then she sank back to her feet. She took a hesitant step forwards and raised a paw. Sylvan, hardly daring to move, stepped down from between the roots onto the little earth platform behind Strife.

' . . . even listening to me. I mean how rude! Kale, I swear I'm going to feed you to a pike . . . '

'Strife,' said Sylvan, not taking his eyes from the female. 'Please could you be quiet?'

' . . . why aren't you listening to me? Aren't you pleased to see me? I'm your sister, although I wish I wasn't, I mean . . . '

'Strife,' said Sylvan.

' . . . brother like you—'

'Strife!' Sylvan yelled. He rounded on her, glaring, shoving between her and Kale.

'What?' said Strife.

'Shut it. Now.'

There was no arguing with his tone. Strife's jaw closed with a snap.

Sylvan turned to the female.

'I'm sorry,' he said. It was all Sylvan could think of to say. He had no more words. He simply gazed at her in silence until Fodur, wet, out of breath, and looking grumpy, threaded his way through the tree roots. He regarded the assembled River Singers. He blinked. Then an expression of delight spread across his pointy features.

'Is Missy Fern,' he said.

Fern raised her chin.

'Hello, Fodur.'

Sylvan closed his eyes. His pulse raced and his breath quivered. He wanted to cry or to shout for joy. He did not dare touch her. She might dissolve away like a mist. He opened his eyes again. She was still there, with her familiar face and familiar scent. It was her. She was different, though. Older, certainly, and she held herself stiffly, with a set to her jaw. She looked harder, and leaner. But it was Fern. His lost sister was standing here, at the edge of the Great River, as real as the night she was taken.

'You're still alive,' he managed.

Fern gave him her smile. The one she kept for the times when she thought he was being stupid. 'Yes. And you're still stating the obvious.'

Sylvan returned her smile, ruefully. He rubbed a paw across his head, feeling oddly bashful. Then he stepped forwards and they touched noses. She put her head next to his and they pressed together. He breathed in her smell, remembered from their times as nestlings. The smell he thought he would never know again. It was her. Fern whom he had wept for. Fern whose loss had always been there, catching him at odd times. Fern who was alive.

He pulled away, struggling to keep his voice level. 'But you were gone. You were dead. The fox took you.'

'Ah,' said Fern. She gestured behind her. 'No. It caught my tail. I lost that, but kept my life. But you . . . the others.'

'Alive. Safe. I did what you said, Fern. I got them to the Wetted Land.'

'All alive?'

'Yes,' said Sylvan. 'All alive.' Then, belatedly, he gestured to his companions. 'And these are Strife and Kale. They're Aven's children.'

Fern began to shake. 'Oh, Sinethis,' she said. She covered her face, turning away. Sylvan swallowed. Fodur gave Sylvan a small smile. Then he moved quietly past to put a paw on Fern's shoulder.

'Is good to be seeing you, Missy Fern,' he said.

Fern gave him a tremulous smile. 'You too, Fodur.' She touched noses with him and let go of a deep breath. 'So,' she said, turning to Kale and Strife, 'you're Aven's children. Kale I've met. So you must be Strife.'

Strife nodded, but said nothing. She looked dumbfounded.

'It's nice to meet you,' said Fern.

'That'll pass,' said Sylvan.

He was expecting Strife to say something, or at least give him a dirty look. But she didn't. She just kept gazing at Fern.

'I see my brother's as charming as ever,' said Fern with a

smile. Strife merely nodded again, wide-eyed. Sylvan wondered vaguely if she was all right. But he had more important things to consider.

'Fern . . . what happened to you? How did you end up here?'

The smile faded from Fern's face. She became business-like.

'Well, it's simple,' she said. 'The fox caught my tail. I broke free and gave myself to Sinethis. The rapids took me, and that's all I remember. I woke up here in this colony.' She made a small gesture at the water and a shadow of grief passed across her features. 'They tell me that I was bleeding and half-drowned,' she continued. 'I nearly died, but somehow I didn't. By the time I recovered it was too late to find you. So I found myself a territory and a burrow. I started my life here.' She gestured at the river again. 'And now this. As you can see, it's been quite a day. I lost my home and all of my neighbours. And then I regained my family.'

Her voice was level, controlled. Sylvan wanted to comfort her, to tell her that it would all be all right. But even as he thought it he felt a coldness at his hind feet as water washed over their little earth ledge. Even after everything, Sinethis was still rising. Fern too noticed it.

'Ah,' she said. 'It seems that Sinethis is catching up with us. Well, we can't all sit here for the rest of our lives. I've already asked Kale this, but I presume that you have some idea of what to do now, since you came all this way to find me?'

Sylvan glanced at Kale who gave a small shrug. Apparently he was out of ideas. Great. The clouds overhead were tinged with red, now. It would soon be dark. *Caught between Sinethis and darkness*, thought Sylvan. *Aren't we always?*

'Right,' he said. 'We can't go anywhere now. It's too risky out there, even in the light. We'll have to wait for dawn.'

'And then what?' asked Fern. 'What happens at dawn?'

'At dawn,' said Sylvan. 'We take you to the Wetted Land. We'll bring you home.'

He tried to ignore the glances that Strife and Kale exchanged. Even Fodur looked sceptical. They had every right to look like that, he thought. They were a long way downflow and the fields were deadly. But Sinethis had brought back Fern, and there was no way she would have done that without a reason. He was filled with a new hope—anything seemed possible. It would all make sense soon. He was sure of it.

'Don't worry,' he said. 'I know what I'm doing. Let's get some sleep and tomorrow we head home.'

They nested for the night in the long grasses at the foot of
the tree. They left the ledge to be claimed by the river. As
exhausted as Sylvan was, he woke before the light. He wasn't
sure what had stirred him from his sleep, but his mind filled
with memories of the Great River and the sound of her song.
Perhaps she had woken him, or perhaps it had been a dream.
In any case he quietly left the others and settled a little way
from the tree, with his back to the river, and simply gazed
out at the lightening landscape. Dawn crept onwards and
hazy features emerged from the darkness. Opposite their
small island the grassy hill rose up to a straggling crown of
woodland. Sylvan narrowed his eyes. Something about that
hill nagged at him, but he couldn't see why. The field was
bare except for a dark line of low shrubs that ran straight up
the centre. The skirting waters curved around the foot of the
field, as if trying to embrace the land. Or crush it.

'What are you up to?'

Sylvan jumped. He had not registered Fern's approach
until she sat down, hesitantly, next to him. He shifted over,
to give her room.

'Not much,' he said. 'Waiting. Thinking.'

'Thinking? You *have* changed.'

He smiled. 'Not really. I used to think quite a lot. I just never told anyone about it.' He gestured at the calm silvery sheet of water between them and the hill. 'I'm thinking about the Great River, and the Wetted Land, and how to get back to it.'

'What's wrong with the way you came?'

'Ugh. Plenty. For a start most of it's underwater, now. And the bits that aren't are too exposed. Also I'm beginning to wonder if it's the shortest route.'

'Oh,' said Fern.

Silence extended between then. Sylvan gazed down at the water, unsure of what to say to this stranger who was also his sister.

'I'm sorry about your home.'

Fern shook her head. 'My home,' she said. 'Maybe it was, in a way. But it never felt right. It was always temporary, somehow.'

'But you had a territory. A life.'

'Yes. But I had no choice. I found a territory because the mink took most of the females. And I spent every day and night watching and waiting for it to return. That's why I never had pups.' She waved a paw at the water that rippled above where her colony had been. 'And I was right not to. I mean, look at this.'

Sylvan said nothing. They were right to have left the Great River, he thought. It wasn't safe, even after all this time.

Fern's voice grew harder. 'They were good Singers, Sylvan. They didn't deserve this. You came back to me, and I'm so grateful. I am. But the price was high.'

'*We offer ourselves as sacrifice*,' said Sylvan. 'Sometimes Sinethis is kind and sometimes she takes us. But she brought us to you. I got my sister back. And soon we'll be in the Wetted Land. She wouldn't bring us together unless there was a way home.'

'Always an optimist.'

'It's the way I am.'

'Oh, we've had such different lives, you and I,' said Fern. But she nestled closer to Sylvan. He rested a paw on her back and they stayed that way, unspeaking as the world brightened around them.

Then Fern said, 'I followed Sinethis, once, you know. Back when I thought I could find you. I followed the river round the base of the hill, almost in a circle. It took days.' She stared away at the memory.

'I didn't find any Singers. Only woods. It frightened me. I didn't know if I was following Sinethis, or only a fantasy. I lost courage and I returned here. I gave in. I suppose you'll think less of me for that.'

But Sylvan was not listening. A thrill of excitement pulsed through him. 'A circle,' he said. 'That's it.'

'What?'

He turned to Fern, eyes shining. 'I've been wondering why this hill looked familiar. I mean I've never been to this bit of river before but I kept thinking that I recognized it. But then I couldn't have because we were so far downflow.'

'Sylvan, what are you talking about?'

'I think this is it, Fern.' Sylvan got to his feet. 'I saw this hill when I was travelling in the Wetted Land. But from the other side. If the river goes in a loop, then we weren't going away from the Wetted Land. We were going *round* it.'

Fern stood too. 'If you're right, that means the Wetted Land is just over this hill.'

'Exactly. Wake the others. We need to feed and get ready.' He grabbed Fern's shoulders with his paws. 'I've got it, Fern. I know how to get us home.'

Fern's expression was stern as she pulled away from his

grip. 'Hang on. You said that last night. You said you knew what you were doing.'

'And I was right, wasn't I?'

Fern gave him a long, hard look. 'I don't know why I keep following you.' Then she sighed. 'I suppose I must trust you. I always did, really.'

'Thank you,' said Sylvan, surprised.

She touched her nose lightly to his, and left to wake the others. Sylvan watched her go. Then he turned back to contemplating the hill in front of them. His eye settled on the long, thin, line of bushes leading almost from the water's edge to the hilltop woods.

A way home, he thought.

Fodur was out of breath, but he limped up the hill with a determined expression. Strife followed, keeping her head down and legs moving. All morning they had weaved upwards amidst the woody stems that Fodur called a 'hedge'. And only now were they nearing the top of the hill. Strife's muscles ached and she was footsore, but since Fodur wasn't complaining she kept her mouth shut.

'Never liked hedges,' said Fodur, pulling up for a breather. He looked at the bushes with distaste. 'I grows up as a hedge rat. I was not sorry when I leaves.'

'I didn't know that,' said Strife. 'What hedge?'

'Heh. Long way from here. Mayhaps I be telling you sometime.'

'Yes, please. When we're back.'

Fodur winked at her. Then he set off once more. Sylvan, Fern and Kale were ahead, picking their path towards the hilltop woods. At Sylvan's suggestion they had strung themselves out rather than move as a group. That way, Sylvan said, they would be more difficult for an enemy to spot. And if some were attacked, the others would have warning. It made sense, but Strife was filled with unease: she had never been this far from water in her life. The morning was quiet and they had seen no enemies, but still she was tense. An attack on this hill would be fatal.

Eventually Strife and Fodur hauled themselves over a lip

to find the others sheltering beneath a bramble, just below the hill's crest. They huddled together, catching their breath and peering at the route ahead. The view was partly obscured by trees and bushes. *Great*, Strife thought. *More woods*. But she could see that these woods were not deep. They were little more than a thin rank of trees, and the branches and leaves were silhouetted against a plain, white sky. A short stretch of shrub-covered ground led to the edge, and there the hill dropped away, down below the horizon. The place bore an unsettling sense of airiness and exposure. They were high above the Wetted Land in places where Singers did not belong. Strife ached to be home.

'Were you right?' she asked eagerly. 'Can you see it?'

According to Sylvan, the Wetted Land lay the other side of this hill, just at the foot. But even now they could see nothing of it. For a moment she thought she had annoyed Sylvan again. He frowned at the bushes and the trees. Then he grinned.

'I don't know,' he said. 'But I can find out.'

Strife followed his gaze. A little way off a fallen branch sagged down, spreading twigs and leaves across the woodland floor. It was still joined to the trunk by a twisted sinew of timber. Sylvan contemplated it with a glimmer in his eye.

'And just how are you going to do that?' asked Fern, suspiciously.

'The branch,' said Sylvan. 'It's exactly what we need.'

The announcement was greeted by a perplexed silence. Sylvan made an impatient gesture.

'Look, we think the Wetted Land is down this hill, right? Well that's how we see. From up there.'

'You're going to climb a tree?' Fern was incredulous. 'That's really dangerous. I mean there might be birds about or anything.'

'It's still early, they won't be flying,' said Sylvan dismissively. 'Besides, don't you want to have a first look at your new home?'

Fern shook her head. Sylvan grinned at her.

'Come on,' he said. 'Race you.'

And with that he wove down through the bushes, scampering among them like an overgrown pup. From the corner of her eye Strife saw Fern with her face in her paws.

'Is a rat saying,' said Fodur from behind them. 'Males is ratlings with longer tails.'

'I have a similar saying,' said Fern. 'It goes: Sylvan's an idiot.'

'Tsk. Is unfair that.'

'Really?' said Fern. 'I'm not so sure. Besides, my saying is more concise.'

Fodur said, 'Heh.' Then he followed down the hill after Sylvan. Strife fell in beside Fern and together they began picking their way towards the branch, keeping to cover.

'So was Sylvan always like this? You know, when you were pups?'

'Oh, no,' said Fern. 'He's grown up a lot. When he was a pup he was *really* immature.' She stepped delicately around the first fallen twigs. 'Oh, for Sinethis's sake. Look at him.'

Strife could just make out Sylvan's form amidst the leaves halfway up the tree branch. He was perched precariously, up on his hind legs and swaying as he gazed down the slope.

'That's Sylvan for you,' said Fern. 'Sometimes he just doesn't see the risks. I think it's because he has faith. In the world, in other Singers, in the Great River. It used to irritate me.' Her expression softened. 'But Sinethis knows how I've missed him,' Fern looked almost bashful. 'Silly, isn't it?'

Strife shook her head but said nothing. She found herself almost in awe of this strange female Singer. She had been through so much that Strife could not imagine. Around her Strife didn't know quite what to say, or how to act.

'By the way,' Fern said, with a severe look

aimed at Strife and Kale, 'if either of you ever tell him that I said any of that there'll be trouble.'

Strife raised her head. 'Oh, you can trust Kale not to say a word,' she said. 'About anything. He never does.'

Kale shrugged then nodded. Fern gave Strife a quizzical look.

'And what about you?'

'I'll do my best,' Strife said seriously. 'But I can't promise much more than that.'

The party reached the tree branch. Above them, just high enough to clear the bushes, Sylvan stared down the hill at the land below.

'What do you see?' Strife called.

Sylvan did not answer. He made a tiny movement of the head as if to shake away a fly.

'Is something wrong?' Strife heard the worry in her own voice. She looked at Kale, Fodur, and Fern. None of them moved.

'Right. I'm going up.'

Before anyone could speak Strife grabbed the branch with both forepaws and scrabbled and clawed her way up through the leaves. At the first fork she paused. The twigs she stood on gave slightly beneath her weight. She looked down and wished she hadn't. She had never been off the ground like this. She scrambled up to the branch where Sylvan stood,

got within
arm's reach
and grabbed his fur.
She clung to him, eyes tight shut.
Then she forced herself to open them.

'Oh, Sinethis,' she whispered. 'What have you done?'

Below them the woodland plants gave way to a thickly hedged field dropping away down to the flat expanse of the Wetted Land. And there it was. Unmistakably her home. But changed almost beyond comprehension. Where once there had been a thriving network of lush dyke edges, a plain of shimmering water now stretched from the base of the hedge to the horizon. Everything else was gone. Fields, dykes, everything. Only the trees still rose up, reflected in the still surface sheen. The stories had come true. Sinethis had sung her terrible song. The Rising had come.

'It wasn't supposed to be this way,' said Sylvan quietly. 'I did everything she asked. She shouldn't have done this. Anything but this.'

Strife tightened her grip on his fur, fighting back an upwelling of grief. Her home. Drowned. Mother. Ivy. She stared at her broken world. Then she released Sylvan and fled down the tree. She barely heard him running down behind her. She hit the ground in front of the others and dashed unthinkingly for the top of the hedge. In two steps, though,

Sylvan had her. He flung his forepaws around her. He bore her to the ground, and held her tight.

'Let me go,' she shouted. 'Mother's down there.' She bared her teeth, squeaking in anger. 'Let me go, I said.'

But Sylvan gripped her tighter. 'Listen to me.' His voice was low and urgent. 'You have to stop, Strife. Think. It's too dangerous. There are enemies everywhere. You can't help them this way.'

Strife pulled herself free and rounded on him.

'And what do you know about anything?' she yelled. 'It's your precious Sinethis that did this. Yours and Kale's. Look what she's done to my home.'

Sylvan flinched as if she had struck him.

'It's my home too, Strife,' he said. 'My brother and sister. My niece. My home.' He shook his head. 'We have to stay together. I can't believe that Sinethis would betray us now. She never has before.'

'She has,' said Strife. 'I mean look at it. How could anyone survive that?'

'I don't know. But I do know that Sinethis has reason,' Sylvan said quietly. 'She brought me back to Fern. It's another test, that's all. We have to be strong enough to face it.'

Sylvan turned to the others.

'It's the Rising,' he said curtly. 'Sinethis has taken the Wetted Land. We'll go down and see what she's left.'

Without a word Fodur scaled the branch, running nimbly up to the viewing point. He stood there for a moment, silhouetted against the clouds. Then he turned and pattered back down the tree. He put his head on the side, considering what he had seen.

'Mayhaps is not so bad as you be reckoning.'

'*What?* How can you say that?' Strife flung a gesture in the direction of her home. 'It's all gone. All of it. How can that be "not so bad"? Or is that some weird rat phrase meaning everyone's dead and our homes are underwater?' Strife slumped to the ground. 'It's horrible,' she said. 'All I wanted was to go home.'

Fodur hobbled over to where Strife lay and stood beside her. He leant down, until his muzzle was almost touching her ear. Then he gently grasped her foreleg and pulled her to her feet.

'On your paws, Missy,' he said. 'This is not how to be a Singer. Is a better way. You stands, yes? You not be giving in.'

Strife climbed shakily to her feet. 'But the water—'

'Is water,' said Fodur. 'Singers is good with water. And is tricksy to see from here. Methinks when we's getting nearer we be seeing things clearer. Be heartful.'

Fern too had cautiously climbed up the branch. Now she came down and stood beside Fodur. 'It's a lot of water,' she said. 'And it looks bad. But I thought I saw plants, Strife. Lines of them above the surface. If there are plants, there's shelter. And if there's shelter then it might be all right.' Fern smiled encouragingly. 'Aven's a tough Singer. If anyone could survive the flood it's her. We can't give up now.'

Strife looked at Fodur and Fern. Both of them had suffered far more from Sinethis than she had. But here they were standing together, full of determination, and comforting her. The thought made her feel unworthy.

Strife took a breath. 'Yes. You're right. I'm sorry. And I'm sorry for what I said. I was upset.' She forced a smile. 'So we'll get down from this hedge and go home. And we'll deal with Sinethis when we get there.'

Kale came forwards and looked at her approvingly.

'Good. I think it's the right thing to do,' he said.

Kale being a know-all. Right. Now Strife was on familiar territory.

'And what do you know?' she demanded. 'Every time you go anywhere trees fall on me and it all goes hideously cow-shaped.' She appealed to the others. 'Look, I'll keep going, but please don't make me follow Kale. He's a disaster. Someone else go first.'

'And that,' said Kale, to nobody in particular, 'is how you know when Strife's all right again.'

'I'm glad to hear it,' said Sylvan. 'We've got a way to go, so let's get moving.'

Then he pattered down through the remnants of the woodland to where the trees met the hedge. Kale followed, and after a moment Fern fell in alongside him, leaving Strife and Fodur alone at the top of the hedge.

'Uncle Fodur,' said Strife.

'Yes.'

'Thank you for looking after me.'

'Is a pleasure. You's OK?'

'Yes. I'm worried, but I'm OK.'

'Is good. I's worried too. But we's nearly there.'

And then they set off together, following the others at a safe distance, moving down the hedge towards the Wetted Land.

On this side of the hill the grasses grew long and luxuriant, piling up in dense swathes next to the hedge. They made it difficult to see. If Strife stood as tall as she could and strained her eyes she could just make out the path of Sylvan's progress, and Fern and Kale's tracks, from the way the plants moved aside at their passing. Eventually, though, she gave up trying and just concentrated on walking. Fodur walked beside her, ears pricked. He scented the breeze often and moved as cautiously as his lame leg would allow. Fodur was taking no chances. Where they were able they stuck to the hedge, weaving among the thick, woody stems. But often they were forced to wade in the sea of grass.

Strife sidled closer to him. 'Uncle Fodur, I think I have something to say.'

'Something to say, heh?' said Fodur. 'Is a surprise, this.'

'Don't be sarcastic,' said Strife. 'It doesn't suit you. Anyway, I've been thinking about Sinethis. I don't like her.'

Fodur angled his head slightly. 'I agrees with you there. But then I's no Singer and I don't expects to like her.' He ducked under a low stem. 'Or for her to like me.'

Strife frowned. 'You mean that I *should* expect to like her? Just because I'm a Singer?'

'You's a Singer. Like or dislike, you follows because you has no choice.'

'Well there should be a choice, I say,' said Strife.

'Mayhaps,' Fodur conceded. 'But who's you going to be asking for it?'

A breeze ruffled through the grasses. Fodur pulled

up short, flinging out a paw. Strife froze. Fodur lifted his nose and took in the scents. He cleaned his whiskers with a forepaw and scented again. Then he recoiled, scrabbling at his nose. For a moment Strife smelled nothing, and then the air carried it to her nostrils: a sharp scent that caught in her throat and started her heart pounding. Weasel. Ahead. Close.

And now the thick flanks of grass and green tangle of hedge turned from reassuring to threatening. The plants surrounded them, blocking everything from sight. The scents were fresh. The weasel could be right in front of them, and between them and the others. Strife turned to Fodur, aghast. But Fodur had slipped from her side and grasped a hedge twig with his forepaws. He pulled himself cautiously upright, standing on his good rear leg. Strife sidled up the low earth bank into the shelter of the hedge. Then she too rose up, moving as slowly as she dared. Her head just cleared the tips of the grasses.

The hill stretched down away from where they stood, grass waving in the light breeze. The floodwaters met the hill at its base, light dazzling from the surface.

Strife strained her eyes. Halfway down to the water was a movement, perhaps a Singer parting the grass. And further up another movement. Kale and Fern. And then, further up still, and moving in efficient straight lines, three separate waves ran arrow-straight down through the grasses, converging on the water voles below. Three weasels, hunting the others.

'Oh, not three,' Strife moaned. 'What do we do?'

'You stays,' Fodur commanded. 'I warns them. I moves.'

And Fodur's paw shoved her back. And then he was past her and away, hurtling down the slope.

'I runs,' he shouted. 'You stays.'

Fodur shot down the field along border of the hedge, yelling as he went, anything to warn the others or to give the enemies pause. Strife stood in dumb shock, unable even to think. But then she realized what Fodur was doing, and what it meant. He might warn the others, but the weasels would kill him.

'No,' she whimpered. 'No, no.'

She began to run. She did not think, but merely reacted. Part of her was terrified, urging her to stop, to go back. But the rest of her simply ran, filled only with the need to get to Fodur. Strife's paws skittered on twigs and slipped on mud. Grasses flattened before her as she sprinted. But Fodur's shouts remained ahead of her, heading deeper into the field, away from the hedge. She followed. She had to catch him. No other thought. And then, abruptly, he was there in front of her, gasping for breath in a small clearing the in grass. He whirled as she approached, glaring at her.

'I tells you to stay.'

Then his attention snapped back to the patch of grass he had been watching. A leaf twitched. 'Gets back, Strife,' Fodur hissed. She did not move. 'To the hedge. Do it. Now.'

Fodur bared his teeth. His ears flattened. Strife backed away, terrified more by the sight of her uncle than by any danger they were in.

She was about to turn when a lean, sandy head popped out of the grasses a mere vole's length from where Fodur stood. It focused on Fodur, and then on Strife. Its mouth opened revealing sharp, white teeth. It gave a chittering call. For long moments nothing moved. No sound. And then two more heads rose up on either side of Fodur. They too stared intently at where he stood. Then the first weasel vanished. There was a movement in the grass, circling round behind

Strife. She pivoted, following the rustle and the movement. She raised her own paws, bared her teeth. It had cut off her retreat. They were surrounded. Strange. It all felt remote, as if she were watching events from a great distance. Strife felt her head come about, following the weasel's progress. She turned until she had her back to Fodur. And then it stopped. She stared, unblinking, at the place where it lurked. It would come through the grass. It would attack.

And then there would be blood.

'Strife.' Fodur's voice. She did not look round. He was at her back, facing the other two weasels. 'When this starts, you run,' he said.

'No. We fight together.'

A soft rhythmic noise. Familiar, but unexpected here. It took Strife a moment to place it. Fodur was chuckling.

'Is the way you is.' The chuckling stopped. 'But is not right here. You run.'

The weasel rose silently up from the grass in front of Strife, just out of striking distance. It stood tall on its hind legs, beadily watching her. Then it began to weave from side to side, eyes locked on the soft tissues of her neck. Its body

swayed hypnotically. Strife knew of this. Weasels liked
to dance for their prey. Singers called it the death dance.
Few ever saw it and lived. Strife's gaze did not waver for an
instant. Even to blink would mean death.

'I'll stay with you,' she said. Her voice was flat, calm.
Level. The weasel weaved in the grass. She watched it.

'You stay we both dies.'
Fodur's words were urgent,
now. 'I's old. I's ready.
You's not.'

She hesitated. A series of sounds in the meadow behind her: a weasel slinking into position in front of Fodur. She did not dare look, but she could imagine what Fodur saw: two more weasels, showing him their dance.

'You's like my own ratling,' said Fodur. 'You run. For me.'

Strife gave a tiny shake of her head. No. The weasel saw the movement, paused for the barest instant in its dance. And then it continued. *Nearly time*, Strife thought.

'Please,' said Fodur. 'For Fodur. Please?'

Maybe later it would feel like cowardice. But right now she knew, with certainty, that it was not. It was the only time Fodur had asked her for anything. His first, and last, request. And she could not refuse.

'Yes. I promise.' The words were almost a sob.

'Thanks you.'

And the weasels came. A shrill scream from behind Strife. She twisted round as Fodur went down, his paws raking and teeth bared, beneath a sinuous shape that snapped for his throat. A stir in the air behind her and she leapt aside, slipping from the reach of her weasel's teeth. She sprang away, bounding forwards even as the third weasel launched past her. Her paws contacted with the ground, her foot twisted over, and she rolled into the thick grass. She came up. She risked a glance. She saw Fodur with a weasel at his back, biting for his neck. The other two weasels, sensing victory, were closing on him, ignoring her. Strife fought down an impulse to run in, to attack the vile creatures and fling them away from her uncle. But if she did that both of them would die. And she had promised. He had made her.

Fodur wrenched free for an instant. He rolled to his paws, and his head came up. He stared past his attackers, eyes fixing on Strife as she hesitated. It was a moment she would always remember, clear as cold water: Fodur panting, bleeding, but unafraid. A hint of a smile.

'Go,' he said. And the weasels fell upon him.

Strife wrenched herself away. She raced down the hill, veering back to the hedge. She met it and followed it, tears blurring in her eyes. She ran wildly, unthinkingly. She did not see Fern and Kale as they sprinted after her, or Sylvan as he joined them. She did not see the floodwater as it lay glistening before her. She did not hear the shouts from behind her, from Sylvan and Fern and Kale, asking what had happened, begging her to stop. She simply ran. And when the ground disappeared from beneath her feet, with a shock of cold, she swam. She swam as though her world were nothing but water to be churned from under her paws. She swam until her limbs shook and her breath burned. She swam until Sylvan and Fern overtook her, pulled her to the side, forced her into a knot of plants.

She stared at their faces, unseeing. Their mouths moved, but she heard nothing. There was nothing for her but loss, like a hole in her that might never be filled. Fodur was gone. The weasels had taken him.

She had done what he asked. She had let him be taken.

Rafts of stems bounced beneath Sylvan's feet and water squeezed up through the matted net of plants. It sloshed over his belly fur and his tail, chilling him. He trod mechanically over what was left of a marshland that once had been filled with River Singers. They had walked all day, aching with fatigue and loss, stopping only to feed. Even then they ate quickly before resuming their travels. Behind them lay the field where their friend had died. Somewhere in the marsh ahead lay the answer to what had become of Aven and Ivy. It kept them moving. Each step brought them closer to knowing whether their shared hope was misplaced. Even Sylvan found it hard to conceive of how anyone could have survived this catastrophe. But still there was hope. Here and there they found fragments of feeding sign, or a fresh dropping. But they saw no other Singers.

The Rising had left a terrible legacy. The tips of the remaining reeds and canary grass waved above their heads. But most of the grasses had toppled, forming lines of smashed-flat plants that lay in tangles where the dyke edges had been. Often even these were submerged, but in places they were sturdy enough to walk on. And beyond these fragile borders the water stretched out, reflecting a broken sky. The rain had ended and a low sun glittered. If Sylvan stared long enough, he could imagine that all the world had turned to sky, and he and the others were floating in it. Only the distant green smudge of trees broke the illusion.

The Wetted Land was coldly beautiful. *Fodur would have liked it*. The thought rose unbidden, and Sylvan put it carefully aside. He separated himself from it, keeping away the upwelling of hurt. Fodur was gone, taken by weasels. That much he had understood. But Strife had said nothing of the rest. She merely walked, following the path because they told her to and eating because she must. Kale stayed at her side, giving her his support, and Sylvan was grateful for that. But even so he watched her, carefully. This world was too dangerous for a Singer to lose herself in grief. When he next called a halt for feeding he drew Strife a little way from the others.

'How do you feel? Are you cold?'

Strife shook her head, and ate a mouthful of grass. She did not want to talk.

'Strife, I'm worried about you.' She gave no sign that she had heard. 'I know Fodur's gone. It hurts. I feel it too. But we're still in danger. I need you to be strong.'

Strife stopped chewing. She put down her grass.

'Is it worth it?' she asked quietly.

'Sorry, is what worth it?'

'Being strong. The sacrifice, or whatever you call it.' Strife raised her head as if it were too heavy for her. But she looked him in the eye. 'You told me that if we fight then Sinethis will give us what we want, that we live our lives as sacrifice to the Great River. And now look.' She gestured helplessly at the water. 'This is what we get? Uncle Fodur's taken and my home is gone. We're dragging ourselves across an empty marsh to find out if my mother and sister are somehow still alive. So I'm asking: is it worth it?'

Sylvan stared down at the canary grass in his paws. 'I don't know,' he said at last. 'I don't think that's up to us to decide. Our only choice is whether to fight or not. That's all we can do.'

'Well I didn't fight,' said Strife bitterly. 'I ran. I left Uncle Fodur to the weasels.' Strife lowered her head again. 'He told me to. And I did it.'

So that was how she had escaped. Poor Strife.

'Then you did the right thing.'

Strife raised her head. 'What?'

'If you hadn't run, both of you would be dead. No one has fought a weasel and lived. We'd have lost you too.'

'But why did it have to be Fodur? I could have fought. Why not me?'

Sylvan wanted to answer that Fodur was an old rat, that he knew about necessity. That he had always made the best of his life, even here in this strange world of Singers. Or he could have said that Fodur had his own ways and his own Taker who had carried him to a land beyond, and that Fodur had kept himself ready. He could have said that Fodur would have given anything for Strife, and done it gladly.

Instead he said, 'Fodur once told me that losing is part of the world. He said that these things are nobody's fault, not even Sinethis's. He was right. And they're not your fault.' Sylvan watched Strife's face. He could not tell if she was listening to him, or if his words were any comfort. 'It was Fodur's choice,'

he said, 'and you did the very best you could. And I will never be anything other than glad that you ran.'

Strife made a small noise. She stared up at the clouds, blinking at the falling light.

'Thank you,' she said.

Sylvan regarded the solemn young River Singer in front of him. A thought came to him that brought a small smile to his face.

'Can I make a suggestion?' he said. 'Look, I can't explain this very well, but if you ever feel that you owe something to Fodur, to his memory, just be the best Strife you can. Make that your gift to him. I think Fodur would like it.'

Strife stared. 'What do you mean?'

Sylvan smiled and shook his head. 'Just bear it in mind.'

From further along the dyke came Fern's voice, calling Sylvan's name. He became instantly alert.

'Come on,' he said to Strife, and moved quickly down the dyke to where Kale and Fern stood side by side, heads together, discussing something in low voices. As Sylvan approached he saw that their path was blocked by a neat heap of feeding sign, topped with fresh droppings. They stood aside.

'It's fresh,' said Kale.

'She's been here today,' Fern added. 'It's occupied.'

A female's territory. A sight from a world that he thought had been lost. Sylvan clambered atop the feeding sign and surveyed the territory. The sight kindled a warm feeling.

'It looks drier,' he said. 'More plants. It looks good.' He glanced up at the sun, now hidden behind a low cloud. 'Look, it's nearly evening and we can't get to Aven today. So let's just—'

'You there!'

A Singer's voice. Female. Not sounding pleased.

'What do you think you're doing? Get off that immediately!'

Sylvan turned to see a large female hustling up to the base of the heap. He quickly scrambled down and out of her territory. The female surveyed them.

'What,' she demanded, 'is the meaning of this?'

'Apologies, Mistress,' said Sylvan. 'We've been travelling for some—'

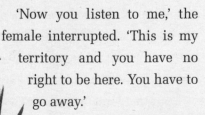

'Now you listen to me,' the female interrupted. 'This is my territory and you have no right to be here. You have to go away.'

'I know, Mistress,' Sylvan tried. 'But yours is the first—'

'I don't care what it is, except that it's mine. Understood?'

'Yes, Mistress, of course,' he said placatingly. 'But we just want to go through.'

She let out an aggressive squeak. 'Go through? Trespassers!' she shouted. 'You're trying to take my babies.'

Sylvan's heart sank. A nesting female. The first Singer they met, and she had pups. Brilliant.

'We're really not,' he said.

'Murderers!' The female's voice grew shrill. Her forepaws paddled at the air. 'Murderers, I say!'

'Look, we don't want—'

'How *dare* you?' Her eyes glittered blackly and she bared her teeth. 'How dare you?' She took a step forward, hackles raised.

Sylvan hastily backed further from the marker, gesturing to the others to do the same. She glowered at them balefully until they were hidden from her by a screen of reeds.

'Nesting,' said Sylvan disgustedly. 'We're not going to get any sense out of her.'

'She doesn't want anyone near her pups,' said Fern, giving Sylvan a reproving look. 'I can understand that. But she could have given us the benefit of the doubt.'

'Well, she didn't,' said Sylvan. 'And now we'll have to swim round her territory.'

He eyed the water unhappily. They were cold and wet enough as it was. Strife, though, was staring at the female, who had climbed up onto her heap of feeding sign so that she could glare at them more effectively. The expression on Strife's face was unreadable.

'Sylvan,' she said. 'I want to have a word with her.'

That did not sound like a good idea.

'We don't want a fight,' he warned. 'Not now.'

'Oh, we're not going to fight,' said Strife, still with an odd look on her face. 'We're going to chat.'

And without waiting for a response Strife walked past Fern and Kale and up to the female. There she rose up onto her hind feet, gazing up at the other. The female glared back.

'You know something?' said Strife. 'I've had enough. I've had enough of walking. I've had enough of swimming. I've had enough of being cold and wet and away from home.' She spoke with a quiet intensity. 'I've had enough of trees and being attacked by cows and weasels and swept down rivers. I've lost my Fodur and for all I know the rest of my family is gone.' Strife's gaze rested on the female's face. 'I am not having a very good time. Can you tell?'

The female nodded, seemingly unable to resist.

'But do you know what the worst thing is?' Strife continued, in the same, quiet tone. 'It's that you are the only River Singer we've seen. You're the best hope we've had. And here you are standing in front of us calling us murderers when all we want is to go home.'

The female opened her mouth but Strife carried on, not even raising her voice. 'And I know that you just want us gone. I understand, I really do. We also want to be gone. I'm sure you and your pups are very nice Singers and everything, but I've got more important things to worry about. My mother is in the marsh, and I need to know if she's all right. It's nothing personal, but I just wish you weren't in the way.'

The female blinked. Then she gradually dropped back down to all fours.

'So I have an idea,' said Strife. 'And it's very easy. If you go back to your nest and stay there we'll pass through. That way you can guard your children until we've gone. And we'll go as quickly as we can, I promise. It won't take long and everybody will be happy.' She opened her paws in supplication. 'What do you say?'

The female looked at the Singers arrayed in front of her, and then back at Strife.

'Yes,' she said. 'All right.'

'Thank you.'

The female took a single step back off the feeding sign. Then she turned and hurried away down the territory.

Sylvan went and stood by Strife. 'That,' he said, 'was amazing. I have no idea how you did it.'

'I talked to her,' said Strife. 'That's what Strifes do best.' Then she gave Sylvan a small, sad smile. 'Shall we keep going?'

They walked long into the next day. Here and there a banktop, tussock sedge, or a woven tunnel of grasses persisted above the water. And in these places there were River Singers. Each new encounter brought Strife fresh reasons for hope. Sylvan and Kale dealt with the males. Strife dealt with the females. Most them just took a few words, but sometimes they stood firm and the group had to swim round. Strife didn't mind too much. Every step brought her closer to home. It was hard to be certain where they were—the marshes were so changed— but the trees had not altered, and each junction of the dykes grew increasingly familiar. She schooled herself to be calm, to keep it all closeted in her heart. Best not to hope too hard. She had no idea what she would do if Mother and Ivy were gone. She would deal with that if it happened. But for now the hope remained.

Eventually they turned a corner onto a dyke that was high enough to have escaped the worst of the water. Two lines of plants ran parallel down the corridor where the banks had been. The stems were woven thickly underfoot, and in places had been fashioned into nests. And set back, a distance from the plants, were familiar stands of dark woodland, the trunks rising up out of the depths. She took in the scene in one breathless instant. Her old dyke. She was sure of it. Further down was her mother's territory. She shared a brave smile with the others.

'Yes. We'll know soon,' said Sylvan. 'But let's go carefully.'

Strife, though, raced ahead, unable to wait. She passed by a tussock sedge that reared up out of the water. At the base, piled high against the dampness, was a boundary marker. Strife ran up to it. She drew its scent down and was rewarded with a glorious warmth of recognition. She stepped away, almost shaking with relief. Unmistakably Ivy's scent. Her sister was alive. Even as Strife thought it, the shape of a Singer stepped into the path.

'Just where do you think—' it began.

And Strife, squeaking with joy, took Ivy clean off her feet.

Ivy went over backwards, borne down beneath the full impact of Strife's enthusiasm. She got her paws up and paddled defensively, but Strife was too happy to notice. She jumped up and down, squeaking, and attempted to fling both forepaws around her sister. Ivy's protests came out in time with Strife's jumping.

'Will—you—please—get—off—me?'

Strife pulled back. She could barely make out the expression on Ivy's face, but she didn't care. Her sister! Alive and well. She grabbed for her, pulled her into a hug and released her.

'Sorry, Ivy,' said Strife. Then she hugged her again. 'But I'm so happy to see you.'

From behind Strife came the sound of Sylvan laughing.

'We'd better give her a hand.'

Strife felt paws grasp her and gently lift her away. Ivy climbed dazedly to her feet.

'OK. OK. I'm calm,' said Strife. 'Let me go, will you?'

'Do you think it's safe?' said Sylvan to Kale.

'No.'

But they released her anyway. Kale pushed gently past Strife and examined Ivy for a moment. Then he smiled.

'You're big,' he said.

Ivy, now she'd had time to take everything in, was staring from Kale to Strife and back again.

'It's really you,' she said. 'You're both safe. Oh, thank Sinethis. It's been so bad in the rest of the marsh. We thought we'd never see you again.'

'We,' said Strife eagerly. 'You said "we". Does that mean Mother? Is she all right?'

'Yes,' said Ivy. 'She's fine.' She turned to Sylvan. 'She stayed in the territory like you said. She kept it safe.'

Strife closed her eyes. She could do nothing but simply be there, revelling in the feeling, and holding it in her heart. They were alive. She was home. Strife heard a sound behind her. She spotted Fern, standing awkwardly at the edge of the run. Of course, Fern! Strife ran back to her, and drew her forwards.

'Ivy,' she said excitedly. 'You need to meet somebody. She's a lovely Singer and she's going to live with us in the marsh.'

Ivy gave her a strange look, but said, 'You're welcome in my territory. I'm their sister, Ivy.'

'Thank you for the welcome, Mistress,' said Fern formally. Then, 'I'm Fern and I think I'm your aunt.'

Ivy's perplexed expression faded. 'Aunt Fern?' She looked sharply at Strife who nodded. 'You mean from Uncle Fodur's stories?'

A stab of sorrow at the sound of Fodur's name. Strife tried to keep it from her face. She did not feel ready for the explanations. Ivy, though, was frowning.

'Uncle Fodur,' said Ivy, glancing from vole to vole. 'Where is he? Is he coming too?'

Strife flinched. Sylvan stepped forwards and put a paw on her shoulder.

'Do you want me to do this?' he asked quietly.

'No,' said Strife. 'But thank you. I should tell her. He was our uncle, and it's best if she hears it from me.'

Sylvan nodded. 'Of course,' he said. 'In that case I'll go ahead, if that's OK, and see if I can find Aven. Come down when you can.'

He made his way off. Kale and Fern followed him.

'Tell me what?' said Ivy as the others slipped away.

Strife took a deep breath and faced her sister. 'Uncle Fodur was taken,' she said.

'Oh,' said Ivy softly. 'Poor Fodur.'

'Let's walk down,' said Strife, 'and I'll tell you about it.'

They walked side by side, and Strife told her about their journey, of the weasels, and how Fodur had saved her.

'So he died. And I'm here. I'm sorry,' said Strife.

Ivy turned to face her. For a moment her expression was unreadable, but then she smiled and pulled Strife into a hug. 'Strife, you have nothing to be sorry about.' Ivy gripped her tightly and then stepped back. She blinked and then looked down at the water, almost bashfully. 'It isn't your fault. I'm just happy you're safe.'

Strife swallowed. She didn't know what to say. 'So is this is your territory now?' she asked, changing the subject. 'It's really nice. Didn't it used to be Mistress Sorrel's?'

'Yes. I was lucky. Mother noticed it was empty before anyone else did,' said Ivy. A quick grin flashed across her face. 'You know what she's like. I didn't even have to fight for it.'

Strife smiled. 'That sounds about right. What happened to Mistress Sorrel?'

'I don't know. An enemy, perhaps.' Ivy gestured at the dyke and gave a helpless shrug. 'In any case it was the Rising.'

Strife gazed at the mess of flattened reeds and water. 'It must have been horrible.'

Ivy nodded. 'Pretty bad. But we escaped the worst, here. Sinethis left us enough to live with.'

They walked on, talking quietly, until they reached the border of Aven's territory. They stopped in front of Ivy's marker, piled high with droppings. Strife felt an odd pang as she breathed in the familiar smells, her sister, her mother. She peered down the dyke at the trees and plants. The water had changed it terribly. But still it was still her old home. Her Mother's touch was visible everywhere, from the ostentatiously huge sections of reed in the feeding sign to the immense boundary markers.

Strife stepped past the markers. Ivy, though, lingered.

'This is as far as I go,' she said in response to Strife's questioning look. 'I've sort of got into the habit of keeping out of Mother's territory.

'Oh,' said Strife. 'Of course.'

Then Ivy said, 'Strife, I'm really sorry. You know. About the night you left. I shouldn't have said those things. I should have helped you. I've been so . . . ' She trailed off miserably.

'Oh, it really doesn't matter,' said Strife. 'And you were probably right anyway.'

She reached out a paw and placed it on Ivy's shoulder. 'None of that's important any more, you know? You're my sister and you're alive and you've got a wonderful territory. I'm just happy to see you again.'

'You too,' said Ivy. They touched noses again. Then Ivy cleared her throat. 'Now,' she said, 'you should go ahead and find Mother. Give her my love. And come back and visit, when you can.'

'I will,' Strife promised. 'It'll be nice.'

Ivy turned away, and Strife ran after Fern and Kale, who were waiting a little way down.

'Ready?' asked Kale. *He looks nervous*, Strife thought. Now they were in their mother's territory Strife knew how he felt.

'Sort of,' said Strife. She took a breath. 'Kale, she's going to kill us. You do know that, don't you?'

'Don't worry,' said Fern. 'I'm sure she'll just be happy you're safe.'

'I wouldn't bet on that.'

'In that case,' said Fern seriously, 'I think I'll let you two go first.'

Sylvan weaved his way down the well-trodden runs towards the heart of Aven's territory. He was filled with impatience to see his sister again. He carried on down the twists and turns until he heard the distinctive crunch of a stem, and the sound of a diminutive River Singer bustling down the dyke edge. And then there she was, staring out at him from between some fronds.

'Sylvan!'

Aven ran up and stopped a bare length in front of him. She stood there, half fearful, half hopeful. She craned to see past him. But the others were still out of sight. She searched his face.

'Good or bad?' she asked softly. 'The news. Good or bad?'

'It's good, Aven. Strife and Kale are coming.'

Aven made a noise like a low sigh.

'Thank you,' she said. She stepped forwards and put her head against Sylvan's. 'Thank you.'

'You're welcome. But we lost Fodur.'

Aven flinched. She backed away. 'How?'

'A weasel took him. He died saving Strife,' Sylvan said.

Aven gazed down at her paws. 'Fodur too,' she breathed. 'Sinethis has a lot to answer for.' She raised her head. 'She took so many of the Folk. But I'll miss him more than any.'

'I know,' said Sylvan. 'He was a finer Singer than all of us.'

'He was,' said Aven. She looked up at the sky, blinking.

Then they heard the noises of the others approaching. Aven rose up for her first view of her children. Strife and then Kale emerged from the reeds and stopped a little distance away, hesitating.

'Hello, Mother,' said Strife, fiddling with her paws. Kale said nothing.

Aven gazed at them in silence. Then she made a sound like a sobbing laugh.

'Oh, for Sinethis's sake. Come here the pair of you.'

And they rushed forwards, nestling against one another, touching noses and grinning in shared delight.

'My babies,' said Aven, her paws around each of them. 'They're back.' She looked up at Kale, who was now bigger than she was, and at Strife who was almost the same size. 'But you're not babies any more, are you?'

Before either of them could answer, Aven rose back to her haunches and whacked each of them, hard on the nose.

'Ow,' said Strife, 'what did you—'

The rest of Strife's words, though, were muffled as Aven grabbed first her and then Kale and pulled them into a tight embrace. Then Aven released them and stepped back with a frown.

'If either of you ever do anything like that to me again you will regret it until the day you die. Understood?' She glowered at Kale. 'I mean what on earth possessed you to run away like that?' Then she rounded on Strife. 'And you, young water vole, over-marked my scent. You're lucky I don't skin you alive and use you for bedding. What were you both thinking?'

From behind Strife and Kale came the sound of a throat being cleared.

'I think I can explain,' said Fern.

Aven froze. She put both paws on Strife's head and stood up, peering past her daughter. Her jaw fell open. She turned to Sylvan.

'But . . . that looks like Fern.'

Sylvan grinned. 'There's a good reason for that,' he said.

'It can't be. She was taken.'

Fern stepped forwards, looking almost apologetic. 'That's what people keep telling me,' she said. She reached around and pulled up her stump of a tail. 'But only a bit of me got taken. The rest is right here. It's me, Aven. Fern.'

Aven said nothing. She simply stared, unmoving, at her sister. She raised her nose and took in the scents, whiskers twitching. She made a tiny movement of the head, like an affirmation.

'Aven,' said Fern cautiously, 'aren't you pleased to see me?'

'Oh, Fern, I'm sorry.' Aven still looked stunned, but she seemed to come to herself. 'Of course I'm pleased to see you. Welcome back, my dear. Welcome to my territory.'

She stepped forwards and reached out a paw. She gently touched Fern's fur, as if to make sure she was real. Then she grasped her sister and held her at paw's length, drinking in the sight of her. Fern closed her eyes, and put her head across Aven's shoulder. Aven pulled her close, and a smile crept across her face.

'It's really you,' she said. 'I can't believe it. My children and my sister have returned to me all in one day.'

'And your brother,' Sylvan pointed out.

Aven gently released Fern. 'Yes,' she said. 'But that doesn't count. There was never any chance of you not showing up.'

'It felt like there was.'

Somewhere overhead a bird called out. The sun slipped behind a cloud and a shadow passed over the dyke. They froze, remembering that they were still in the open. Aven became instantly business-like.

'Right,' she said. 'We can't all stand around like this. We better get to my tussock. There's probably enough room in there.' She frowned at the group. 'And then I have a *lot* of questions that need answering.' She gave Fern and Strife an appraising look. 'And when we've finished talking, we'd better see about getting you two somewhere to live. As lovely as it is to have you both back, we can't have three females in one territory. It'll lead to arguments and Folk being injured. By me, mainly.' She grinned at Fern to show she was joking. 'Mistress Mallow's territory has been empty for a day or two. If we move fast I think we should be able to get hold of it. It'll be perfect for you to share.' Aven took a deep breath. 'Right. Now that's all sorted out we'd better get under cover.'

And she turned and pattered happily away down towards her tussock. Sylvan followed, and after a moment Fern appeared beside him.

'What do you think?' asked Sylvan. 'Happy?'

'Oh, very. It's wonderful,' Fern said. 'Although this is a side of Aven I haven't seen before. She's quite, um . . . '

'Territorial? Yes, I know.' He stepped around a water-filled hole in the grass. 'You've got to pity the other females.'

'Definitely,' said Fern. 'Especially because "other females" will include me if she gets her way.'

'You'll be just fine. Most of it's an act.' He watched Aven's tiny frame bustle away. 'Most of it.'

Morning sun crept into the burrow. It flowed over Sylvan as he sat in the entrance. The sun had a thin quality to it, though, as if the receding floodwater had carried away some of its warmth. This early the insects were not out, and the birdsong too was strangely sparse. The marshes were as quiet as he had ever known them. He heard the patter of Kale's feet in the burrow behind him.

'Mother said you'd be here.'

'She was right.' Sylvan moved over a little, leaving space for another Singer in the entrance. 'We've still a little time before we leave, and the sun's good. Care to join me?'

Kale squeezed in next to Sylvan and they sat side by side. Soon they would go out to feed, and then the open marsh, with all of its intrigues and dangers, beckoned. Aven's territory was lovely, but he and Kale had their own way to make.

Kale said, 'I haven't heard her for ages.'

Sylvan knew who he meant without asking. 'No. Sinethis is keeping quiet.'

'What's it like? You know, living without her.'

'Nice, actually. Peaceful.'

'Oh.' Kale breathed a sigh. 'I'll have to get used to it.'

Sylvan smiled. 'Don't worry, it's not hard. And no doubt she'll interfere before life can get too boring.' He gave Kale a dry smile. 'Probably just as you're beginning to enjoy yourself.'

A soft splashing came to them from outside the burrow, followed by Aven's voice.

'Right, you two. There'll be enough time for all that male chat when you leave. I think it's high time that you came down and said goodbye properly. I've just checked the place over, and there are no enemies.'

Aven had been up long before them. Maintaining her boundaries was something she took seriously even with her daughters living next door. Sylvan ran down the gentle slope to his sister, with Kale just behind. Aven stood amidst the mud-coated mess of stems and leaves that the falling waters had left. She had spent days creating new runs and markers. She still had a big job ahead and Sylvan did not envy her.

Aven ran an expert eye over the pair of them and gave them an approving nod.

'Well, you'll do.'

What for, Sylvan didn't know. But it was always nice to have a positive assessment.

'Sylvan,' said Aven, 'look after Kale for me. I know he looks big, but he's still just a pup.' She turned to Kale. 'Kale, the same goes for him.'

'Thanks,' said Sylvan. 'I knew I could rely on you to make things unnecessarily sarcastic.'

'Well, that's what I'm here for,' said Aven. 'But I mean it. Look after yourselves. Right?' She looked Kale up and down one last time. 'Not bad,' she said. 'If my next litter turns out so well I'll be a proud mother. Now,' she continued, 'Strife's meant to be meeting you at the marker to take you down to Fern. Whether she'll be there or not is anyone's guess, but that's the plan.'

Aven touched noses with Sylvan and then Kale. Then she turned away a little. 'I can't have two useless great males like you clogging up my territory. Time for you to go. Be off with the pair of you.' She took a few steps towards the burrow and paused. 'But don't be away so long this time.' Then she disappeared into her burrow without a backwards glance. But both Sylvan and Kale caught the quaver in her voice. They exchanged a heavy look and set off down the dyke.

They wandered along Aven's territory as far as the patch of loosestrife where Sylvan had saved Strife and Kale from the stoat. Just beyond it lay the boundary marker. One half was neat and strongly laced with Aven's scent. The other an untidy heap of hastily arranged droppings and smells. That alone was sufficient to mark it as belonging to Strife. And, of course, Strife herself was nowhere to be seen.

'Not surprised,' said Kale.

'Nope. Me neither.'

They eventually found her peaceably grazing in a stand of iris just outside her main burrow.

'Oh,' she said with a full mouth. 'I was supposed to be somewhere to meet you or something, wasn't I?'

'Don't worry,' said Sylvan. 'We found you anyway.'

'Good point.' Strife swallowed her mouthful. 'So, you're off then? And I see you have stupid with you.'

'Yes, Kale's coming with me, at least for the first bit.'

She grinned. 'I wasn't talking to you.'

'Very droll vole,' said Sylvan. 'So now we're here do you want to escort us off your territory? Or would you prefer we just find our own way?'

Strife waved a paw vaguely down the dyke. 'You don't need me to show you the way. It's off down there somewhere. You'll find it.'

Sylvan surveyed Strife's new home, nodding approvingly at the plants that move quietly in the morning air.

'This is a good territory, you know. And a fine Singer in it.'

'Thanks,' said Strife, looking pleased. 'Are you going far?'

'Who knows? But you have another uncle I need to look in on. He lives over the other side of the marsh. Orris probably survived just fine, but I'll be worried until I check.'

Strife nodded. 'Well, make sure you look after Kale. He may be a moron, but he's my moron, and I want him back some day.'

'I'm not a moron,' said Kale.

'Yes you are. You've been nothing but trouble ever since we were pups. I've never met such a complete idiot in my entire life. In short,' she concluded, 'you're a twit.'

'And you talk too much.'

They regarded one another for some moments. Then Strife said, 'I'm really going to miss you.'

'You too.'

THE RETURN

Strife pulled him into a hug. Then she released him. She waved her paw again.

'That way,' she said. 'Go on. Go and be a bonehead somewhere else.'

Kale gave Sylvan a resigned look and set off down the run. Sylvan followed, smiling.

'And remember to look out for owls,' Strife called after them.

They moved together down the dyke edge towards Fern's territory. The sun rose a little further, finding a renewed strength that filtered down through the grasses. But the shadows still remained chilly. As they passed into them, Sylvan was reminded of something he had once heard, of a frozen time when the waters set like stone. But it was probably just Singer's talk. And even if it wasn't, Sinethis would be with them, a mother to her children, just as she had always been. The thought was half reassuring, and half warning. *Fight or be taken.* He pushed through a fringe of sweet-grass. *That is her way.*

And then they left the shadow and the sun shone warmly on their backs. The waters washed gently against the dyke edges and everything around them was green and gold. The marshes lay ahead. Sylvan grabbed for a sweet-grass stem and chewed it as he walked. He savoured the sweet-bitter taste of it. *Not bad*, he thought. He breathed a lungful of fresh morning air and remembered that the world could be wonderful.

EPILOGUE

Strife rose cautiously up out of the grasses, just far enough to have a clear view. She checked all around. Nothing to be seen. She scented the air, but aside from her mother's smell on the boundary mark there was nothing. She hadn't really thought that there would be predators out so early, but it was best to check. Besides, it wasn't really predators that Strife was worried about. She dropped to all fours and slunk up to the mark. It was half hers, and there was no real need for sneaking, but somehow it felt appropriate. Just beyond the droppings and the little mud platform, the last of the loosestrife waved in the breeze. Strife's favourite flowers. And growing in her mother's territory, where Strife wasn't really supposed to go, these days.

Strife lifted a paw. But then, from back down the dyke behind her, came the sound of plants stirring. She froze, instinctively. And relaxed when the sound was followed by a jostling noise and a high-pitched giggle. She rolled her eyes. Oh. The pups again. Really, those two were a complete pain in the tail. Why their mother couldn't keep them closer to the burrow she had no idea. Strife was sure that when *she* had been a pup she would never have dared to stray too far from the nest. She waited with her best attempt at a severe expression as the scuffling sounds got closer. Eventually a pair of young Singers rolled into view, scrapping and bickering. They pulled up short at the sight of Strife's glare.

'And what do you think you two are up to?'

The larger male blinked solemnly at her for a moment and then his features split into a grin.

'Morning, Strife,' he said cheerily.

'That's "Mistress Lou" to you, young Fodur,' said Strife severely. 'And what have I told you about coming into my territory?'

'You said we were welcome any time, and you didn't

want to be like the other grown-ups,' said the other male.

'What? I did *not* say that!'

'Did too.' He turned to his brother. 'She did, didn't she?'

'Yes, I heard her.'

'I did not,' said Strife indignantly. Then she caught herself. Who was the adult here? She pulled herself up to her full height and stalked up to the small male until she was glowering down at him.

'Burr,' she said, 'don't argue with me. You might be family but don't think for a second that that will stop me from eating you.'

The tiny male swallowed and took a step back. *That's better*, thought Strife.

'You wouldn't eat me, would you?' said Burr, looking nervous.

'Only because you'd taste nasty.' She smiled to soften the words. 'I've had bigger morsels than you for breakfast and still had room for lunch. Hey! Fodur, ask permission before you do that.'

Fodur, who was impudently stuffing his face with canary grass behind her back, dropped the stem he was holding.

Strife shook her head. 'Honestly,' she said. 'You were named after one of the finest rats any of us ever knew. Try to behave like it, will you? And look, does your mother know you two are here?'

The pups glanced at each other and then nodded with two perfect expressions of wide-eyed innocence.

'Thought not. Come on, let's get you home before Fern comes looking for you.'

Ignoring their protests Strife escorted the two males back through her territory to where her section of dyke met Fern's. Fern certainly had her paws full. In addition to these two she had three females. They would be a full-time job even if Fodur and Burr behaved themselves. Which they didn't. Fern said that her litter would have been perfect except that both males had turned out like Sylvan. But when she said that she smiled and ruffled the fur on their heads. Fern seemed more than happy, but as far as Strife was concerned pups were still just pups: irritating and unruly and a complete waste of valuable time.

Fodur, walking beside her, looked thoughtful. 'Strife?' he said eventually.

'I don't know anyone of that name.'

'Sorry. Mistress Strife?'

EPILOGUE

Strife sighed. 'Mistress Strife' was probably the best she would get.

'Yes, Fodur. What can I do for you?'

'Why were you up near Mistress Aven's territory?'

'I go there sometimes,' said Strife, giving him a look, 'when I want to mind my own business.'

'Oh,' said Fodur. 'It's just Mother says that if you keep going into Mistress Aven's territory there'll be trouble.'

'Humph.' Strife kept her gaze firmly on the run she was following. 'Not as much trouble as you'll be in if you keep coming into mine.'

They walked in silence until the edge of Fern's territory came into view.

'Here you are. Off you go, and give my love to your mother.'

'Yes, Strife.'

Fodur scampered off. Burr, though, stared at the boundary mark that Strife and Fern shared. Neither female really bothered to keep it maintained, just adding a new dropping of scent every so often. But for the pups this was an important place.

'You don't *really* mind us coming to see you, do you?' he asked.

Strife smiled. 'Not really. But don't tell anyone, OK?'

'That's good.' Burr grinned. 'See you, Strife.'

And he ran off after his brother, completely ignoring the words that Strife yelled after him: 'That's Mistress Lou to you!'

Strife made an exasperated sound then turned and headed back up through the heart of her home. As she walked she kept one eye on the dyke. The water was down to the lower entrances, now. Sinethis had retreated, slipping away and out of the Wetted Land. She had returned to her place, and the marshes had once again become safe backwaters. But they were different, now. They were emptier and humbler. The minds of the Singers were filled with fresh memories, of water and of drowning. They would pass the stories to their pups. And those pups would tell their own children, and soon enough the stories would begin to fade. And then the Singers in the Wetted Land would forget about Sinethis.

But Strife wouldn't forget. The River Singers were meant to be children of the Great River. All around were the lingering signs of Sinethis's rage: in the dried residue of the flood, the empty feeling of the marsh. The Folk would survive. That's what they did. But what sort of mother would do this? For a moment the sky darkened. A few raindrops spattered into the dyke, making a soft splash. A tiny, singing note rose up from the water and chimed somewhere within Strife. Then it passed. Strife found herself nodding. She looked around at the fresh green plants, and for a moment she felt that she understood. It wasn't a matter of approving or not. Sinethis was as she was. *She shelters us in her waters and burrows. She rises and dashes us.* Sinethis would not change. All the Singers could do was live with her, the best they could.

And Strife was doing just that.

She arrived at the far end of her territory and gazed over at her mother's patch of loosestrife. *Trouble*, she thought. *But so worth it.* And, with a mischievous grin, she was across the boundary and in among the flowers. Most of the petals had gone, now, and greenish seeds swelled among the yellow and purple. But they were still lovely. She breathed their scent and closed her eyes.

Perfect, thought Strife.

Tom Moorhouse lives in Oxford. When not writing fiction he works as an ecologist at Oxford University's Zoology Department. Over the years he has met quite a lot of wildlife. Most of it tried to bite him. He loves hiking up mountains, walking through woods, climbing on rocks and generally being weather-beaten outdoors.

MESSAGE FROM TOM

If you're reading this then it's possible you haven't realised that the story ended a few pages ago. You probably need to turn the light off and get some sleep—it's late. Alternatively, of course, you might be here hoping to learn a bit more about writing, water voles or general author type stuff. And if that's the case then you've come to the right place! Over the page I've written some fun facts about water voles (so you can impress your friends with your in-depth knowledge of one of Britain's rarest rodents), but first I want to tell you something about what it's like being an author.

One question I am asked quite a lot (almost as much as "Do you know where the post office is?", "Have you got the time on you?" or "Why don't you stop writing and give me a hand with the hoovering for a change?") is where I get my inspiration. And every author I've ever spoken to has been asked the same. There are a number of possible answers, from the very simple to the quite personal and complicated. As an example of the simple answer, I spent eight years of my life as an ecologist studying water voles in the wild. And so when I sat down to write some animal adventure stories, using water voles for *The River Singers* and *The Rising* was the natural choice. You see? Simple.

The problem is, though, that the simple answer just tells you the facts. It doesn't really explain why I, or anyone else, would want to write something in the first place. It doesn't tell you what inspired me to write. I think the real answer is different. For me the real answer is that writing a book means taking all sorts of thoughts and feelings, and bits of knowledge and events from my own life, and mixing these up with different parts of my personality to tell a story about how I see the world, and what I think about things. So I tell stories full of characters and adventures, hoping that somebody (and yes, I hope that somebody is you) will read *The River Singers*, or *The Rising* and find themselves caught up in a strange tale that came out of my head about some small animals that I spent eight years studying. If that happens it means that you have understood a bit about who I am, and about the water voles that have been such a large part of my life. And if so that's a wonderful, wonderful thing. It means—in however slight a way—that we have shared something. And you can believe me when I tell you that's all the inspiration I need.

FUN FACTS ABOUT WATER VOLES

VOLE FACT # 1: Water voles are rodents, the group of mammals that also includes mice, rats, lemmings and capybara (which are the world's biggest rodents, and weigh more than you do). All rodents LOVE to gnaw on things, and have two pairs of front teeth (one pair at the top and bottom, called incisors) that continually grow, so they never wear away. Water voles actually use their teeth for digging as well as gnawing. So if you ever see a water vole burrow, just think that it was dug by chewing. Urgh. Gritty. Their teeth are bright orange, not because of inadequate dental hygiene but because that's the colour of the super-tough enamel that covers them.

VOLE FACT # 2: Water voles are almost entirely vegetarian. They are known to eat at least 227 different kinds of plants in Britain. They are like the world's smallest cows, and they need to eat constantly just to keep going. They

leave piles of chopped up stems all over the place—we call these stems 'feeding sign', and they're usually full of iris, or reed, or canary grass. Every so often, though, you might find feeding sign with crayfish claws in it, suggesting that these otherwise diligent vegetarians might have lapsed for an hour or two. (Crayfish, apparently, is the water vole equivalent of a bacon sandwich. Mmmm. Bacon.)

VOLE FACT #3: Female water voles are territorial. This means that they have a length of riverbank (or dyke, or lake edge) that contains all of the food and burrows they need to live and raise their young. It also means that they need to defend their territory against other females who might want to pinch it. Female water voles spend a lot of time and effort making sure that other females keep off their patch (see latrines, below, and feeding sign, above—both are signals that say "Oi, get stuffed, this is mine").

You may notice in my books the females don't like each other very much, and you can see why: it's difficult to be nice to your neighbour if you think she'll run into your home and change all the locks when you go out.

VOLE FACT #4: Male water voles are not territorial and play no part in raising pups. They aren't tied to a particular family or territory but instead have large ranges that overlap with lots of females' territories—so they can keep an eye on lots of females at once. If this sounds like an easy life, bear in mind that all the other males want exactly the same thing, and wouldn't be too chuffed with other big, hunky blokes hanging around. So there is quite a lot of fisticuffs. Also there is no guarantee that the females will be pleased to see the males: if they are raising pups they are ultra protective, and therefore very violent. One way or another male water voles spend most of their lives trying to avoid being beaten up, either by bigger males or by enraged females.

VOLE FACT # 5: Water voles have flank glands that give off a smell peculiar to the vole in question. They leave this scent at territorial markers—called "latrines"— by scraping their glands with their hind legs and then

drumming their feet down
onto flattened piles of their
own droppings. This is just one of
the reasons that there will never be a
superhero called "Vole Man"—just think
of the mess.

VOLE FACT # 6: For water voles an American mink
is essentially the Terminator. Water voles have been in
Britain for thousands of years, and despite a whole suite
of enemies (fox, heron, stoat, weasel, owl etc.—if it fancies
a small, squeaky meal, it will eat water voles) they have
been doing just fine. In fact until the 1970s they were found
nearly everywhere there was water, and were a common
sight when you went for a walk. Mink were brought over
less than 100 years ago, so we could farm them to make
fur coats. (That's right, both mink and water voles are the
ultimate fashion victims.) They promptly got out and since
then we have lost over 98% of our water voles. Against
mink water voles have no defence. And why would they—
they would never have met a mink if we hadn't got involved.
So water voles will continue to be in big, big trouble as long
as the mink remain.

WANT TO GO BACK TO THE SOURCE?
READ ON FOR AN EXTRACT OF THE RIVER SINGERS

PART 1
THE GREAT RIVER

The dawn was grey and the waters quiet. Sylvan was the first awake, lying with his brother and sisters in a pile of cosily intertwined limbs. Their breathing lulled him even as lightness spread up the tunnel and into the chamber, bringing with it the scent of morning. He yawned. He opened his eyes. He grinned. Today was the day. At last.

Sylvan extracted himself, ignoring the others' sleepy protests, and sat with twitching whiskers at the entrance to the chamber. He should wait for them, he knew. They were supposed to go out all together. But the air stirred with a promise of new things and, with a final glance at his siblings, he stole away down the tunnel, paws padding on the soil. He had known the way for ages now. A left, a right, loop around a knot of roots, then pause at the place where the roof had fallen. One eye to the sky. Quiver. Listen. Check the scents. Then onwards and downwards to the lower places, the entrance to the Great River and the gateway to the world.

With each downward step the light grew brighter and the air fresher, more exhilarating. Another turn, a slight rise. And there she was: the Great River. Her waters, lapping against the family's trampled little platform, were bright through the shade of the tall grasses. She filled him with her vastness, her movement, her song. He felt the stirrings of hunger, the desire to dive, to twist, to flow with her. He hesitated, one forefoot raised, everything urging him out and into the world.

'And what exactly do you think you're doing, young vole?'

A paw was on his tail, pinning it to the floor.

Sylvan froze. He placed his foot hurriedly back onto the ground. As his mother removed her paw he turned, radiating guilt.

'Nothing.'

Her whiskers were stiff with disapproval. 'What have I told you about coming here?'

Sylvan dropped his gaze. 'I'm not allowed to. It's dangerous on my own,' he recited.

'That's right. So what are you doing?'

'Just looking.'

'Hmm. Well, that's just as well. Because any of my offspring stupid enough to think that he could go off exploring on his own would find himself in here gnawing nettle roots while the rest of us were outside. Understood, Sylvan?'

'Yes, Mother. Sorry.'

'I should think so.' She surveyed the dejected water vole in front of her. 'I tell you what: since it's a nice calm day, and seeing as I promised, I don't see why we can't still have that little trip out. Together.'

Sylvan's head came up. 'Really?'

'Really. Now why don't you go and wake the others?'

'Yes, Mother. It's—' He was almost dancing on the spot, torn between his desire to stay near the water and the rush to fetch his siblings.

She turned. 'What, dear?'

'It's wonderful,' he blurted.

She smiled, showing her strong, orange teeth. 'Yes, dear, it is. Now go.'

Sylvan scampered back to the nest where his brothers and sisters were still sleeping. He rushed into the chamber and pawed at the flank of the nearest.

'Come on, Fern. It's today.'

'G'way.' Her voice was muffled, cuddled up against her sister.

'But it's today.'

'Please go away.'

He clambered over the heap and shook at his brother's shoulder. 'Wake up. We're going out today.'

Orris opened his eyes. 'Out?'

'Yes, out.'

'Don't want to. Leave me alone.' Orris huddled in on himself.

Sylvan gave him a disgusted look and turned his attention to Aven's diminutive frame, giving her a brotherly kick on the haunch.

'Come on, Tiny. Mother's promised we're going out today.'

Aven gasped and sat upright, pawing the sleep from her eyes. She groomed a little, setting her fur straight. She blinked her black eyes into focus.

'Sylvan,' she said sweetly, 'if you ever call me that again I'll gnaw your ears off.'

Sylvan grinned. 'You'll have to catch me first.'

'Or wait until you're asleep.'

He thought about it. 'Good point,' he conceded. 'Can we go out now?'

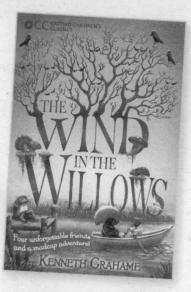

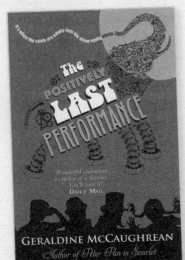